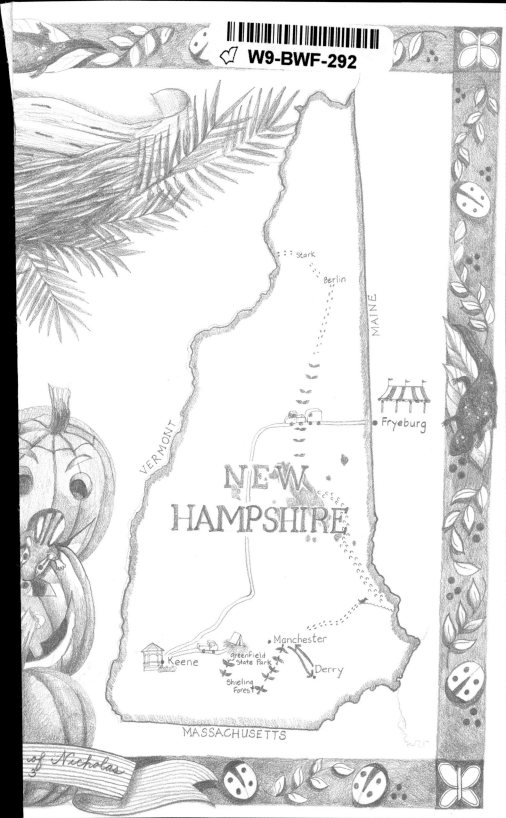

Nicholas

A NEW HAMPSHIRE TALE

by Peter Arenstam

illustrated by Karen Busch Holman

mitten press

All inquiries should be addressed to:
Mitten Press
An imprint of Ann Arbor Media Group LLC
2500 S. State Street
Ann Arbor, MI 48104

Printed and bound at Edwards Brothers, Inc., Ann Arbor, Michigan.

10   9   8   7   6   5   4   3   2

Library of Congress Cataloging-in-Publication Data

Arenstam, Peter.
Nicholas : a New Hampshire tale / by Peter Arenstam;
illustrated by Karen Busch Holman.
p. cm.
Summary: Nicholas the mouse's search for an important family journal
takes him across the diverse state of New Hampshire, where exciting adventures
and new animal friends await.
ISBN-13: 978-1-58726-521-1 (hardcover : alk. paper)
ISBN-10: 1-58726-521-4 (hardcover : alk. paper) [1. Voyages and travels--Fiction.
2. Mice--Fiction. 3. Animals--Fiction. 4. Adventure and adventurers--Fiction.
5. New Hampshire--Fiction.] I. Busch Holman, Karen, 1960- ill. II. Title.
PZ7.A6833Nj 2009 [Fic]--dc22
2008048541

Book design by Somberg Design
www.sombergdesign.com

Chapter One

Nicholas, a small brown mouse, and Edward, a chipmunk, raced from booth to booth at the Fryeburg Fair. There were so many tidbits to eat and things to see. There was popcorn and fried dough. Pretzels and cotton candy. There were people, prizes, and livestock.

"Come on, let's get something to eat, Nicholas," Edward said.

"Edward, I think we'd better wait until dark," Nicholas said, trying to catch his breath. "There are too many people wandering around now."

Edward stopped behind the wheel of a food cart. "But I am so hungry," Edward said. "Can't we just get some fried dough?" He eyed a slice of the warm bread that a child had dropped under the counter.

"People get jumpy when they see little animals like us around. Let's go into that barn for a while. I saw some friendly looking goats when we first arrived," Nicholas said.

Nicholas and Edward had traveled to the fair in a trailer with a gray Percheron horse named Austin. In the last year, the mouse and the chipmunk had traveled a long way together. They were in search of Nicholas's family journal and his cousin Francis. Francis and the journal were located ahead of them, somewhere in the state of New Hampshire. The two small animals were looking for clues that Francis had left behind.

Nicholas and Edward followed a girl carrying a pail of soapy water into the barn. The girl set her bucket down next to a pure white goat. The two friends hid in the straw.

"Here you go, Coconut," Tracy said to the goat. "Let's get you looking your best." When she finished, the goat's hair glistened like a freshly frosted cake. "You're about as pretty as a picture," she said. "Now, try and stay clean. I want to see some of this fair. I'll be back in time for the judging." Tracy left and Nicholas popped out from under the straw.

"Hello, there," he said. "Do you mind if my friend and I stay here with you for a while?"

The goat stood on her hind legs in surprise. "Oh, my,

oh my, you startled me! Please, don't raise any dust. I am ready to compete and I can't have my coat getting dirty," Coconut said.

"Heavens, no, that wouldn't do at all," Edward said, popping up next to Nicholas.

The goat pulled at the rope holding her in the stall.

"A beauty such as you needs the utmost care," Edward continued.

"How many more of you are in that straw?" the goat asked. "Are your paws clean?"

"It's just Edward and me," Nicholas said. "We have come all the way through Massachusetts and Maine."

"I am Edward," the chipmunk interrupted, bowing low. "I'm keeping an eye on this young mouse."

"We look out for each other," Nicholas said. "I'm trying to find my cousin Francis. Edward heard he is in New Hampshire, and we're looking for clues to help find him."

A gang of boys raced into the barn, each holding a wand of pink cotton candy. Nicholas hid behind a bale of hay. The boys stopped at Coconut's stall.

The goat kept one eye on the boys and talked to Nicholas. "You're not in New Hampshire yet. That's where I live. We will be going back there at the end of the week."

"You will? Can we come with you?" Nicholas asked, leaping forward.

"Please, mind my freshly shined hooves. I do wish those boys would be careful with their cotton candy." Coconut skidded about, trying to protect her fur.

"What my young friend wants to know," Edward said, "is would you be good enough to give us a ride to New Hampshire? That is, after you win your competition."

"Yes, yes, I'll get you a ride to New Hampshire, if you'll stay away until after the show."

"You are so kind," Nicholas said. "We'll leave you to finish getting ready." Nicholas and Edward scampered out from the stall and among the feet of the boys.

"Hey, look at that," one boy said. "It's a mouse and a chipmunk together. Let's get them."

Nicholas and Edward circled around trying to avoid the young boys. They ran between the legs of the very clean goat.

"There they go!" one boy said.

Waving their cotton candy, the boys leapt after the small animals.

"No, no, no," Coconut bleated, seeing the pink fuzzy candy. She reared up on her hind legs. The boys in front tried to stop, but the boys in back plowed into them. They all landed in a heap on top of the goat. She was a ball of pink cotton candy and straw. The boys ran from the barn.

"What have you two done?" the goat gruffed. "Look at me! It will take hours to get this cleaned off."

"I am so sorry," Nicholas started to say.

"I have to get washed up. Go find Tracy and bring her back now," Coconut said. She tried to shake the mess out of her white hair.

"I'll find her," Nicholas said.

"Nicholas, we were on our way to New Hampshire, remember?" Edward said.

"You can forget about your ride to New Hampshire unless you find Tracy," Coconut said.

Nicholas and Edward ran off looking for the young girl. They had no idea where to start. They knew Tracy and Coconut could be their ride to New Hampshire, but first, they had to help undo this mess.

Chapter Two

The fair was busy when Nicholas and Edward left the goat barn. They didn't know where to find Tracy. They dodged among people's feet from the Ferris wheel to the lumbermen's displays. They were ready to give up when they heard the clomp, clomp, clomp of hooves.

Nicholas saw a huge gray horse ambling along. A driver holding his reins walked behind. "Austin, is that you?" Nicholas asked, running up to the huge horse. "We need your help."

"Hello, Nicholas," the horse shook his mane and jangled the tack. "Are you enjoying the fair?" The horse walked on as Nicholas talked.

"We've only been here one day and we already have a big problem," Nicholas said. He explained about the goat and their ride to New Hampshire.

"Hop up, Nicholas. You will have a great view from atop my head," Austin said. "I'll help you find the girl."

"I don't know, Nicholas," Edward said. "I never did trust horses. They're so big and everything."

"Don't be silly, Edward. You know Austin from our ride in the horse trailer," Nicholas said. He clambered up the horse's leg and along his broad speckled back.

"Nicholas, that tickles," Austin said. He shook his head again, hiding Nicholas in his mane.

"I'll go tell Coconut you're still looking," Edward said. "She may need to be comforted," he added.

"Come on, Austin, let's look over by the baking contest," Nicholas said. The powerful animal left his driver behind. Nicholas spied a young girl, carrying a red-and-white spotted ribbon in her hand, watching the judges testing slivers of pie.

"There she is," Nicholas squealed. Austin muscled his way forward. Nicholas tried to think of a way to get the girl's attention.

Austin neighed and stomped his hooves. The crowd was getting nervous. Austin reared back, lifting his front hooves off the ground and Tracy looked up. She thought the gray-and-white spotted horse was beautiful. Everyone else backed away. As the horse came down to the ground, Nicholas launched himself off the horse. He leapt toward Tracy's hand.

Nicholas grabbed the red-and-white ribbon as he flew through the air. He held the cloth between his teeth and ran for all he was worth.

"Come back here!" Tracy exclaimed. She took off after Nicholas. The horse driver caught up with Austin and led him away to his barn. Nicholas, with Tracy running behind, raced toward the goat barn.

At the end of the week, Nicholas and Edward thought it safe to visit Coconut again. In the goat barn, she stood proudly in her stall. Pinned to the post in front was a bright blue ribbon. Coconut spied the two animals and called them over.

"Come here, I have something to say to you two."

Nicholas and Edward thought Coconut was going to be mad at them for what had happened.

"I have you two to thank for this ribbon. I took first place in the show. Tracy worked so hard to clean me up after the cotton candy mess that I never looked better."

"I am so happy for you, Coconut," Nicholas said. "I'm sure Tracy is very proud of you."

"Yes, I must say," Edward added, "you are the most beautiful goat I have ever seen. Now, about that ride to New Hampshire, what do you say?"

"You can come with us if you like," Coconut said. "But where in New Hampshire are you going?"

Nicholas and Edward looked at each other.

"We don't know," Edward said. "I heard that Nicholas's cousin passed that way but we don't know where to look for him."

"Maybe I can help," Coconut said. "Ever since you told me about looking for your cousin and the clues he left behind, I have been thinking about something."

"What is it?" Nicholas asked.

"When we first got to the fair, I found this in my stall." Coconut shuffled around in the straw and dragged out a small piece of paper rolled up like a drinking straw. "It was next to a small knothole in the wall of the barn. I know mice must come and go through the hole," Coconut said.

"Let me see that," Edward said. "If that is a clue, I am sure I can figure it out." Edward unrolled the paper. "Well, let me see," he started. "This should be quite simple. I imagine it is a kind of note, written in a foreign language, no doubt."

"Edward, perhaps I should take a look. After all, it was written by a mouse," Nicholas said. He took the paper and held it up to the light. He was silent for a few minutes. "This first mark is a mountain. This other group of marks means 'stands alone,'" Nicholas said. "But I don't understand what he was trying to tell us."

"That's what I have been pondering while standing here in my stall," Coconut said. "I could see the mountain mark, there, but the other marks didn't make sense. Now I think I know what he meant."

"Yes, of course, that means mountain," Edward added, unnecessarily. "I saw that right away."

"New Hampshire is full of mountains," Nicholas said. "Which one could he mean?"

"That's just it," Coconut said. "The second part you explained is the clue I needed. Monadnock is a native word that means 'mountain that stands alone.' Mount Monadnock is a mountain near where I live. Francis must have headed there."

"You could be right, Coconut. Francis must have gone there to hide out and watch for me," Nicholas said.

"It all makes perfect sense now," Edward said. "I was just coming to that conclusion myself."

"You two should get in my trailer now," Coconut said. "We are leaving for Keene soon. Hurry now!"

Nicholas and Edward ran to the small animal trailer parked next to the barn and snuggled down in the fresh straw. They were on their way to New Hampshire, getting closer, Nicholas hoped, to finding his cousin and the journal.

Chapter Three

The trip to Keene, New Hampshire, from Fryeburg, Maine, was a long and bumpy one. Tracy and her parents rode in the old green pickup. The trailer they towed behind carried Coconut and her two new friends. To pass the time, Nicholas told Coconut about their adventures.

"I live on a farm in western Massachusetts," Nicholas told Coconut. "My mom and dad kept a journal of old family stories. One day, it started to rain. It rained for a whole week. Dad tried to protect the journal but it was ruined in the flood."

Coconut slowly chewed on some hay as she listened.

"We lost everything in the flood. My parents needed to rebuild our house. I volunteered to go find my uncle who had a copy of our journal and bring it home."

"That's where I came into the story," Edward interrupted. "You see, I was traveling, enjoying the sights of our state, when I, hmmm, ran into Nicholas."

"An angry bobcat was chasing you," Nicholas chuckled. "I had to fish you out of a river, if I remember correctly. We became fast friends after that."

"Yes, we have had some exciting times together," Edward said.

"But we are still looking for my family journal," Nicholas added. "I have been searching everywhere, through Massachusetts and Maine. Now, if we can find my cousin Francis, I can copy the journal and head home."

"Why is he running away with the journal?" Coconut asked.

"That's what we don't know," Nicholas said. "He took off with it suddenly last year and no one knows why. We need to find him and help him if we can," Nicholas said, looking at Edward.

When they reached the farm, Tracy led the goat out of the trailer and put her in the barn. Nicholas and Edward followed behind and tried to stay in the shadows.

It was fall and cold at night. The clean straw and Coconut's warm body made a comfortable place to sleep.

Nicholas and Edward spent some time on the farm with Coconut. They were still looking for a way to reach Mount Monadnock.

"I am worried about finding my cousin," Nicholas said to Coconut. "It is getting late in the year. The weather is colder every day."

"Yes, it can be dangerous climbing mountains in New Hampshire this late in the year. It might start out looking like a nice day, but clouds will roll in and soon it is snowing. If you are going to find your cousin on Monadnock, you will need to find him soon," Coconut said.

Their chance did come just a couple of days later. Tracy and her family had been busy for the past week. Nicholas had watched as Tracy's father brought a trailer load of small pumpkins into the barn. Everyone in the family carved as many as they could. The pumpkins stacked up in the trailer. Nicholas asked Coconut what they were doing.

"There is a big festival in town this time of year. People bring as many pumpkins as they can to the town square. The pumpkins are set out in rows on the ground, on benches on the sidewalk. Some are stacked on staging high up in the air."

"What are they all for?" Nicholas asked.

"Do the people sit down to eat them all?" Edward wanted to know.

"It is a big contest," Coconut said. "The town of Keene tries to break the record for most carved pumpkins in one place. People from all over the state come to Keene to see the pumpkins."

"We will find someone who is going toward Mount Monadnock at the Pumpkin Festival," Nicholas said to Edward. "If we keep our ears open, I'm sure we will find someone to give us a ride."

The two animals watched as Tracy's father loaded carved pumpkins onto the trailer. Tracy and her mother helped. When all were packed, they climbed into the green pickup. Nicholas and Edward ran for the trailer and jumped into two hollow pumpkins stacked in the back.

Nicholas waved through the jagged eye of a pumpkin face. "Good-bye, Coconut! Thank you for all your help with the clue."

Edward, a bit plumper than Nicholas, managed to only get his arm out the pumpkin's crooked, smiling mouth. "Good-bye, my dear! Best of luck to you at next year's fair."

The trailer jolted down the long dirt driveway and out to the street. The pumpkins settled in the trailer. The pumpkins containing the two animals rolled over on their sides and down into the pile. Nicholas and Edward would have to stay where they were until the pumpkins were unloaded.

Chapter Four

The green pickup rolled into the hilly town of Keene. They parked near the town green. Tracy and her parents unloaded the carved pumpkins. Tracy grabbed the pumpkin holding Nicholas and her mother picked up the pumpkin holding Edward. Both animals popped out at the same time. Tracy and her mother laughed aloud.

Edward had spent his trip eating. The insides of the pumpkin tinged his face orange. Stringy pumpkin pulp covered his head. "I think we have a little chipmunk clown," Tracy's mom said. Nicholas had stuffed as many pumpkin seeds in his cheeks as they would hold.

The two friends quickly jumped down. They scampered around the stacks of pumpkins and through the people's legs. Edward shook off his stringy wig. Nicholas spit seeds as he went. They hid behind a tower of pumpkins on the town green.

"I am not used to being a laughing stock," Edward said. He scrubbed his face with a fallen maple leaf.

"Well, at least we are in town," Nicholas said to Edward. "We have to look for a ride to Monadnock, remember?"

"Of course, of course, my little friend," Edward said. "Just leave it to me."

"Let's look together," Nicholas suggested. They wandered around town looking at the sights, while trying to stay out of view. The trees on the hills surrounding the town were ablaze with color. Orange, red, yellow, and brown leaves competed with each other for attention.

Everywhere they went stacks of carved pumpkins lined the streets. Visitors arrived in town. Couples wandered up and down the street. Families tried to keep little ones from climbing on the pumpkins. Grandparents bought cider and cookies for their grandchildren.

Edward, always hungry, sniffed at the warming cider and wanted a taste. He approached the table selling cider. He stood on his hind legs to get a better view. "Nicholas, doesn't that cider smell heavenly?"

Nicholas was interested in the next table that held a big stack of freshly fried donuts. A family approached the table.

"These donuts will make a good snack for tomorrow," the mother said. "Let's get a half-dozen for our hike."

Nicholas perked up his ears. He wondered where the family would be hiking. Edward stood on a great tall pumpkin, trying to get a better sniff of the hot cider.

The two daughters looked at Edward. Each held a cup of cider in their hands. They tried to entice him to come closer. The mother put down her canvas tote bag to pay for the donuts. "We are going to Monadnock in a few days. Will these keep?" she asked the donut seller.

Nicholas couldn't believe it. This family was going to the mountain soon. Nicholas hopped in the canvas tote and buried himself under a sweater in the bottom of the bag.

The girls, still playing with Edward, didn't notice the mouse. They were trying to get the chipmunk to hop in a pack basket of their own. Edward, who was happy for the attention of the two girls, inched closer to the basket. The girls quickly scooped him up. They shut him in the pack basket and ran down the sidewalk after their mother.

Nicholas, snug under the sweater in the tote bag, wondered what happened to Edward. The chipmunk nibbled an apple in the pack basket and thought about how clever he was to find this food.

The family with the two girls was camping in Greenfield State Park. They had driven over to see the

Pumpkin Festival. Now they headed back to their campsite. The tote with Nicholas and the pack basket with Edward were in the back of the car.

At the campsite, the girls hurried to build a fire and bundled up in warm clothes. The late fall temperature was dropping. The family sat around the big fire at sunset and talked about climbing the big mountain.

Nicholas took advantage of the dark to climb out of the tote. "Edward, where are you?" Nicholas called. He peered into the pack basket and saw his friend curled up in a ball, his tail wrapped around his body. An apple, with a ring of teeth marks right around it, lay next to him.

Edward opened an eye. "Were you calling me, Nicholas? I was just catching up on my sleep. We have a big day ahead of us. We'll be climbing mountains again, eh, Nicholas? Remember the time we hiked up Wachusett in Massachusetts?"

"It's cold, Edward. Let's try to get near the fire."

Nicholas and Edward crept nearer the fire. The family all sat on one side, their feet stretched out. Nicholas scrambled on to a pile of wood. He warmed his paws near the flames licking up into the night.

Edward scrambled up next to Nicholas on the wood-pile. "There you are, Nicholas. We need to stick together on dark and cold nights like this. I'm going to get some sleep. Wake me up if I miss anything."

Edward curled up at Nicholas's feet with the flickering light warming his fur. Edward dreamed of warm summer days and napping in the shade of a big pine tree back home.

Chapter Five

It was still dark when Edward woke up. It was cold and all that remained of the fire were just a few embers glowing in the fire pit. He was alone. The family had gone into their tent hours ago, and Nicholas was nowhere in sight. Edward heard a gnawing sound off in the dark. He started to look for a safe tree to climb.

The gnawing and scrabbling sound came closer. Edward headed straight up a pine tree at the edge of the campsite.

"Oh, hello there," a rather plump porcupine said. "Didn't mean to startle you," he said, looking up at Edward. "I do so love a salty axe handle. I can't help myself really." He dragged the small axe along to the dying fire. "My name's Perry."

"Yes, well, that's fine. Say, have you seen my friend Nicholas? He's a small brown mouse. He's about this big," Edward gestured with his paws. "He has a skinny little tail."

"Well, you know there was a bit of a ruckus here about an hour ago. I'm surprised it didn't wake you."

"A ruckus, you say? No, I must have missed it," Edward said. "What happened to Nicholas?"

"Let me see. First, a skunk came wandering along looking for dinner. They're not against eating a small mouse now and again, you know," Perry said.

"Don't tell me," Edward interrupted.

"No, no, I saw the little mouse wake up but the skunk ran off at the sound of coyotes prowling in the woods."

"Coyotes," Edward said. "That would be even worse."

"Yes, it would, but the coyotes never got to the campsite," Perry said. "I guess the sound of a bobcat snarling in the woods scared them off."

"A bobcat," Edward said. He was very upset now. "I had a close call with a bobcat myself a while back. They're nothing to take lightly."

"Yes, I guess that's what the man in the tent thought.

He woke up and shined a very bright light into the forest. It did the trick. The bobcat must have hightailed it out of here."

"What became of my friend Nicholas?" Edward asked again. "You never mentioned what happened to Nicholas."

"Oh, him, he scampered into the tent when the man came out with the flashlight. I guess he was cold. It can get pretty chilly here in New Hampshire late in the fall."

"Yes, so I see," Edward said. "Now I have to sit here and wait for Nicholas to come out."

"Best of luck to you, I must move along. There are plenty more campsites to visit, even this time of year." Perry waddled off.

Edward sat up in a crotch of the tree waiting for sunrise and Nicholas to emerge from the tent.

When the sun rose, obscured by the tall trees, Edward heard stirrings inside the tent. At first, there was quiet murmuring inside. Loud squeals and laughter followed. Children burst from the tent holding up a wool sock.

Nicholas peeked out of the top of the sock looking warm and comfortable. Edward shivered with cold. He scrambled down the tree and hid near the woodpile. The rest of the family emerged from the tent, dressed for a hike. While the girls ate their oatmeal, Nicholas found his friend sniffing around the cook stove.

"Hello there, Edward. Isn't it a lovely morning? I

had the best night's sleep. I heard the girls say we are going to Monadnock today."

"Well, I am glad you slept well, Nicholas. I was very worried for you all night. I didn't sleep a wink."

"You should have come in the tent with me. The girls are very friendly. Are you cold?"

"Never mind that now," Edward said. "How are we getting to the mountain?"

"The girls are taking me with them in a pack basket. Their mom said I could come along. I'll be able to ride all the way up the mountain. I can look out for my cousin the whole way. Won't that be great, Edward?"

"Ah, yes, I guess it will," Edward said. "But what should I do? I won't be able to keep up with you climbing up the mountain."

"I see what you mean, Edward. I'll tell you what, while the girls are feeding me breakfast and their parents are busy getting ready, you can hide in the car. When we get to the mountain, you jump out and wait in the woods near the trailhead."

"When I find my cousin Francis, we'll look for you near the base of the mountain."

"I suppose I can catch up on my sleep. After all, I didn't get much last night, you know," Edward said.

"Yes, thank you Edward, for watching out for me. Now hurry and get in the car. We will be leaving soon."

The family busied themselves about their campsite packing lunches and water bottles in the car for the ride to Monadnock. Edward found a spot near the spare tire in the back. Edward watched from the car window as the girls fussed over Nicholas, feeding him bits of bread and orange slices.

Edward also noticed Nicholas would ride in the backseat between the two girls. They had made a comfortable nest using the wool sock tucked into an empty oatmeal box. At least, Edward thought, holding on as they bumped along the road, they were on their way to Monadnock. He was sure they would find Francis among the granite boulders of the old mountain.

Chapter Six

It was a beautiful fall day. The family parked at the base of the mountain. While everyone was busy putting on packs and retying shoes, Edward hopped from the car. Nicholas watched him blend in with the fallen oak, beech, and maple leaves that carpeted the forest floor.

Nicholas, safe in the pack basket, scanned the trail looking for signs of his cousin. The first part of the trail was easy walking. The girls laughed and sang as they walked.

Soon the family reached a steeper part of the mountain. The trail was a jumble of granite boulders. The girls slowly scrambled up and over each one. Looking up, the trail of gray stones looked like a tumbled, dried streambed to Nicholas.

Everyone halted for lunch on a sunny ledge with a view of the surrounding countryside. The trees were full of color. The sky was brilliant blue. In the distance,

farmhouses dotted the hills with white. The girls set
Nicholas down on the warm granite. They had brought
peanuts and raisins for his lunch.

While the girls shared a donut after their meal,
Nicholas heard the sharp cry of a blue jay deep in the
woods. Blue jays, Nicholas knew, kept an eye on things
in the forest. Maybe the jay would know where to find
his cousin. As he scampered off, the girl's father called
out, "Come back to the trail, girls. That little mouse can
take care of himself."

Nicholas was now alone in the woods on the mountainside. He could not hear the blue jay any more.

Except for the wind in the trees, it was quiet. Nicholas hadn't seen any other animals. He wondered what had happened to Edward.

Nicholas sat on a mossy stone munching on an acorn. Two blue jays fluttered into the branches of a red oak tree. "Well, there he is!" one blue jay said to the other. "I found him, Harry."

"Are you sure it's him, Warren?" the second blue jay said.

"I don't know," Warren said. "Maybe it's not Nicholas. Let's keep looking." The two jays flapped off the branch.

"Hey, wait a minute," Nicholas jumped up. "I am Nicholas. It's me," he shouted at the birds. Warren stopped in mid flight. Harry crashed into him. Both birds tumbled to the ground. The birds were a ball of blue-and-white feathers, leaves, and acorn caps.

"Are you all right?" Nicholas asked the tangled birds.

"Did you say your name was Nicholas?" Harry asked from the bottom of the pile. "I told you, Warren. I told you it was him."

"Get off my beak," Warren squeaked. "I heard what he said. Harry, did you have to stop in mid-flap like that?"

"Why were you looking for me?" Nicholas tried to brush the leaves and twigs off the birds.

The two jays settled their feathers. Harry tried to help Warren get up.

"Please," Nicholas asked, "why were you looking for me?"

"I will tell you if my brother here leaves me alone," Warren said. Harry opened his beak to say something, but looked away at an acorn instead.

"Do you have a friend who's a chipmunk?" Warren asked.

"Yes, I do."

"Aha, I told you," Harry said, quickly dropping the acorn he had been trying to crack. "I knew this was the mouse we were looking for."

"Yes, I have a chipmunk friend named Edward," Nicholas said.

"That's the chipmunk's name," Harry said. "I could not remember his name but, when you said it, I remembered. Edward, that's right," Harry said, stepping in front of Warren and Nicholas.

"Yes, Harry, I know that's his name. I'm trying to talk to this mouse," Warren said. He stepped around his brother again. "I'm trying to tell Nicholas that his friend needs help."

"Edward needs my help?" Nicholas said. He tugged on Warren's wing. He tried to get his attention.

"Now look," Warren said. "We have upset the mouse. I told you I would tell him what's wrong without upsetting him."

"Why will I be upset?" Nicholas asked. His friend Edward had plenty of scrapes before, but he always managed to come out all right.

"Now, don't be upset, Nicholas," Warren said. He scowled at his brother. "We were talking with Edward. He had something for you but he couldn't catch up with you on the mountain trail."

"That's when we tried to help," Harry said.

"We said we would fly him up the mountain. I'm a strong bird," Warren said. "I knew I could do it."

"And I was going to help," Harry said.

"What happened?" Nicholas asked. He was getting impatient with the jays. "Where is Edward?"

"Well, we took off all right. Edward doesn't like to fly so he was kind of squirmy, but he stayed on my back."

"I was just asking if Warren was getting tired," Harry said. "I guess I flew too close to Warren."

"Edward kind of jumped when Harry flew too close," Warren said.

"Did Edward fall?" Nicholas asked. He was afraid to hear the answer.

"Well," Warren paused. "He started to fall. A red-tailed hawk swooped in close and snatched Edward just as he tumbled from my back," Warren said, all at once.

"A red-tailed hawk," Nicholas said. He knew this could be trouble for any small animal.

"Now, listen, Nicholas. We chased that hawk halfway to the Shieling Forest. Edward was okay when we turned back to look for you. I'm sure he will be fine," Warren said.

"That's right," Harry said. "We'll take you to the Shieling Forest. It's not too far from here."

Nicholas didn't hesitate. He jumped on Warren's back. The two birds took off and flew east. Nicholas looked down and wondered if Francis was back on the mountain. He couldn't look for him now. Edward needed his help. He had to rescue his friend, and then they could return to find Francis.

Chapter Seven

Nicholas held on tightly to the blue jay. The big bird, Warren, was strong and flapped his wings mightily. Harry, his brother, flew close by, ready to take over when Warren tired. Nicholas had flown with many birds in his travels. This was the scariest ride he had so far.

"Are you sure you are all right?" Nicholas asked Warren. He seemed to be slowing down. They were getting closer to the treetops.

"Oh, I'll be fine. I just need to rest a bit."

They brushed over the tops of tall pine trees. Nicholas gripped the jay with his small paws.

"Be careful," Nicholas said. He tried to look for his friend among the pines. From above, the trees formed a green carpet, dense and impenetrable.

"Do you want me to take over?" Harry asked his brother. He swooped in close and Warren veered away.

"Steady now, Harry, stay clear. You can have a turn in a minute."

"I'm ready," Harry said. He flew close to his brother. Their wings brushed against each other. "Just say the word and I'll take over whenever you say."

Warren tried to right himself after Harry's wing swept by his face. "Careful now, I can't see a thing. Do you want me to drop our little friend?"

"I won't let anything happen to him," Harry said. "We're almost to the forest, and I haven't had a chance to carry Nicholas. Don't you trust me?"

"Of course I do, Harry. You remember what happened the last time we tried to help a little mouse. We never did find the poor little guy."

"That wasn't my fault," Harry said. "You said I could carry him. That sneaky red-tailed hawk swooped in on us. He made me drop him."

Nicholas had been trying to look for Edward when he heard the birds mention a mouse. "Where did you take the mouse?" Nicholas asked. "What was his name? Was it my cousin? I have been looking for him for a long time."

"Now, what was his name?" Harry said. He flapped in close to his brother again.

"Be careful, Harry," Warren said. "I think his name was Fred, or Frank, or something?"

"Was it Francis?" Nicholas said. "What happened to him?"

"Yes, that was his name. It was Francis," Warren said. "I don't know what happened to him. Harry was carrying the mouse, and we were traveling toward the Shieling Forest when the red-tailed hawk showed up."

"I didn't see him coming," Harry said. "I tried to avoid him, but that bird is fast."

"Harry set him down in a pine tree in the forest, and we had to take cover ourselves," Warren said.

"That's right," Harry said. He swooped in, imitating the red-tailed hawk. "He flew at us from above, and I had to drop down to a tree to save Francis." Harry dove on Warren as if he was the hawk. Warren wobbled again. He was getting very tired now.

"Watch out," Nicholas shouted. It was too late. One minute he was riding on the back of a wobbling blue jay and the next minute he was clinging to the top of a pine tree. The tree swayed from his weight. "Warren, help! Come back here!" Nicholas watched as the two blue jays flew on arguing.

Nicholas looked out from the very top of a tall pine. The old tree stood above the rest growing in the forest. He swayed back and forth in the breeze. The sweeping branches wafted the scent of pinesap by his nose. The pine needle tassels tickled. Nicholas didn't dare let go.

He was in a patch of trees growing next to an old field. The sun was setting and the forest below was in shadow. The old tree groaned and popped as it swayed. Nicholas didn't want to stay up on top of the tree all night.

Carefully he turned himself around and faced the ground. Slowly, one paw at a time, he crept down the tree. Some parts of the tree were sticky with sap. As he inched his way along, he put his paw into a fresh drop. Nicholas was stuck. He could not go back up and he couldn't go down any more.

He tugged on his paws stuck in the golden resin. He could hear the red-tailed hawk calling out in the fading light. He did not want to be stuck up here where the hawk could see him. He tugged again. His paw popped free, and Nicholas tumbled down the trunk, bouncing off branches as he fell. He landed with a crunch on a big pinecone hanging from a bobbing branch.

With the weight of Nicholas and his sappy paws, the pinecone bounced a few times and then broke off the branch. The cone fell and Nicholas held on tightly. He landed with a thud. The pinecone collapsed under him and cushioned the fall.

The flattened cone slid down the pine needle–covered hillside. Nicholas rode it like a sled. Ahead, a pair of huge boulders appeared. Nicholas tried to stop. He dug in with his paws. He ended with a "thunk" against the side of the first boulder.

Nicholas was sore and scared. The light of the setting sun couldn't reach to the forest floor. It was cold at the base of the two stones looming over the little mouse. After all the shouting and excitement of traveling with the jays, everything was still. Nicholas was tired and scared, so he curled up in a tight ball and slept.

Chapter Eight

When Nicholas awoke, it was dark. The forest was quiet. His head hurt. From where he lay, he stared up the side of two of the largest boulders he had ever seen. They looked like two stone mountains dropped from the sky into the middle of the forest.

Nicholas heard a slow, steady thumping. The noise started, then stopped. After a moment, he heard the thumping again. It came closer. Nicholas rolled off his flattened pinecone and tried to hide under the edge of the overhanging stone.

From this dark spot, Nicholas watched a snowshoe hare sniff the air. Its fur was mottled. It was starting to turn from the brown it was in the summer to the white of winter. The hare hopped toward a clump of ferns. She nibbled, then sniffed the air again. She looked toward the shadow concealing Nicholas.

"Who's that hiding in my dooryard?" the hare asked. "Francis, is that you? I thought you had gone days ago?"

"I'm Nicholas," he said, scurrying out of the shadows. "You know Francis? He's my cousin. I need to find him."

"Hello, little mouse. I'm Sandy. I knew your cousin. He stayed with me here in my home under this stone for a while."

"Where is he now?" Nicholas asked. "I have come all the way from Massachusetts looking for him. He was in Maine, but left suddenly, and I don't know why. I've lost my friend Edward. He and I have been traveling for a long time now. I'm tired and miss my home." Nicholas sat down, worn out, sore and lonely. The hare hopped up next to the sad mouse and nuzzled him with her soft cheek.

"There now, little mouse, don't you worry. You can rest a while. You are safe here. This is the Shieling Forest. The word shieling means "shelter," and I will protect and help you if I can," Sandy said.

"Sandy, where is my cousin?" Nicholas asked.

"Francis was here only a few days ago. You aren't far behind him. He was trying to protect something when I met him."

"It must have been the journal." Nicholas jumped up and looked at Sandy, "Did he say where he hid it?"

"No, he wouldn't tell me. He just said that he would learn the secrets."

"What does that mean?" Nicholas asked. "The journal tells stories of my family's past. What secrets?"

"He was upset and guarded," Sandy said. "He wanted to prove the importance of his family history."

"It is important," Nicholas said. "It is important to our family. I met a friend in Massachusetts who told me we all play a part in history, no matter how small."

"History is about everyone's story," Sandy said. "Seeing my young ones grow up and move on to start their own stories is my part of history. We nibble on the grass and plants. We help new plants grow. Our young rabbits grow up and have bunnies of their own."

"It is a story repeated throughout nature," Sandy said. "Mice, foxes, deer, and chipmunks all can tell a story like that."

"Chipmunks!" Nicholas shouted. "I almost forgot about my best friend Edward. A red-tailed hawk took off with him toward this forest. Have you heard anything about him?"

"Let me see," Sandy said. "I did hear some commotion last night. It sounded like shouting and the cry of a hawk."

"That must have been Edward. Where was the noise coming from?"

"Let me think a minute," Sandy said. She sat back and scratched herself with her hind foot for a moment. Nicholas watched her impatiently. "I was nibbling on some wild mint down by the stream," Sandy gestured with her nose down the hill.

"After that, I hopped up the hillside along the old stone wall," Sandy said. "Toward a nice little patch of wintergreen I know about. Yes, that's right. I definitely heard the noises up by the ridge."

"Let's go then. I am sure it was Edward. He can kind of make a lot of noise when he is in trouble," Nicholas said. Sandy hopped after Nicholas, who took off toward the ridge. The ground was rising as they made their way through the forest. Once the area was all farmland and stone walls, but the trees had taken over again.

They arrived at the base of a big pine tree. Even in the dark, Nicholas could see a dark bowl shape of twigs and bark near the top of the tree. "That must be the red-tailed hawk's nest," he said quietly to Sandy. "Do you think the hawk is still around?"

"If she is, she won't be for long. It is time she headed south for the winter."

"We can't wait for the hawk to leave her nest for the winter. If Edward is still around, I need to find him now." The two animals crept away from the tree and hid behind the stone wall to come up with a plan.

Chapter Nine

Nicholas and Sandy sat behind the stone wall in the dark and listened to the night noises. Nicholas thought about the time he and Edward lived in a stone wall near the Quabbin Reservoir in Massachusetts. Nicholas missed his friend. He could almost hear Edward's voice.

Nicholas couldn't wait any longer. "I have to get up there and help him. He must be stuck in the nest."

"I have many friends in the forest," Sandy said. "Stay here and I will go get help."

Sandy didn't let Nicholas ask more questions. She bounded down the hill into the darkness.

Nicholas didn't like the sounds coming from the nest. "I need to see what is going on," Nicholas said to himself. Quiet as a mouse, he reached the base of the tall pine tree. He was a good climber. The rough bark of the old tree was easy to grip with four paws.

Nicholas inched his way up the tree. He paused, resting on the big branches. He looked up. He didn't want to alert the hawk if she was in her nest. Nicholas knew hawks had very good eyesight and could hear noises from far off.

Nicholas could see the nest was made of big twigs, bark, and moss woven into the shape of a lumpy bowl. Nicholas called his friend. "Edward," he whispered. "Are you up there?" Nicholas looked up at the nest.

A little fuzzy brown head poked out over the side of the nest. "Why, Nicholas, is that you? I had hoped to surprise you, but I seem to be in a bit of jam."

"Edward, what are you doing in the hawk's nest? Is she around?"

"Oh, heavens, no," Edward said. "She went off hunting at dusk. I have been sitting in the tree all day waiting for her to leave."

"Why are you still in the nest, Edward? Don't you want to get away before she comes back?"

"I have something for you, Nicholas. You won't

believe it when I show you what I found on Monadnock." Nicholas scrambled into the nest. The two animals hugged.

"Edward, I was so worried. Two blue jays told me a red-tailed hawk had carried you off. I thought the worst. What are you doing up here?"

"That's just the thing of it, Nicholas," Edward said. "I found a clue from your cousin. I was standing in a clearing at the base of Monadnock when this very rude hawk swooped down and grabbed the birch bark with his talons."

"A clue?" Nicholas asked. "What does it say?"

"That's just it," Edward said. "I was trying to read the clue when the hawk took it. Well, I wasn't about to give up so easily, so I hung on to the bark and we flew all the way back to her nest. I think the hawk was more interested in lining her nest than in me."

"The hawk didn't see you?" Nicholas asked.

"The birch bark folded over and covered me up. I managed to jump off and hide under a branch when we landed at the nest."

"Show me the clue," Nicholas said. "Maybe we can read it and leave before the hawk gets back."

"There you have it, Nicholas. I have been trying to pull the clue out of the nest ever since she left. The clever hawk has woven it right into the twigs. I have been tugging and pulling, trying to get it out. I don't want to tear it. We need to hurry as there is no telling when she will return."

The two animals looked out at the sky. It was dark and a cool wind blew up the valley. The time had passed when hawks cruise for food. They knew she would be back before long.

"Maybe, now that you are here, we can free the clue together," Edward said. Edward bent up a twig and Nicholas tried to work the piece of birch bark free. Bit by bit they worked at it. Nicholas kept popping his head above the rim of the nest looking for the hawk. Edward moved another twig. Nicholas tugged again.

Edward lifted the last twig holding the birch bark in place, and Nicholas gave one more tug. It came free and Nicholas fell back against the side of the nest.

Edward started to laugh, but when he opened his mouth, they both heard the sharp cry of a hawk. It was not far off.

"Edward, we have to get out of here. The hawk is on her way back."

"Not so fast, Nicholas. I'll climb over the edge. Hand me the birch bark.

Edward was over the edge of the nest and had his hands on the birch bark when the hawk swooped into the nest. Nicholas let out a squeak and crawled out of the nest. He followed Edward. The hawk had one talon on the birch bark. She lifted up in the air, dangling the birch bark and the two frightened animals holding on to it. Nicholas was thinking about letting go and making a jump for the tree when a family of purple finches fluttered overhead.

HERE IS A NOTE FOR YOU
to see
A stonewall divides a good
neighbor from me
Boyhood fun is found in a
birch tree
The house of a poet is where
I will be.

The finches were used to defending their nest and eggs from hawks. They circled over the big bird, calling out to each other. One finch flew in close from one direction. The hawk swerved away. Another finch swooped in from another direction. The hawk swerved the other way. Nicholas and Edward held on to the birch bark and swung from side to side.

"Hold on now," one finch said. "We'll get her to let go." Three finches came at the big hawk from three different directions. The hawk, tired of the argument over one piece of birch bark, let go. Nicholas, Edward, and the birch bark tumbled down out of the sky.

Chapter Ten

Nicholas and Edward rolled over and over with the birch bark as they fell from the sky. Edward shrieked. Nicholas shouted. They both tried to grab more tightly onto the bark. They managed to slide up on top of it. The finches swooped in and each grabbed a corner and flapped their wings faster than a hummingbird.

The birch bark formed a hammock. Nicholas and Edward stayed in the middle and held on to each other. The wind whistled by their ears. At last, they landed with a thud on the ground. The four birds, the two animals, and the birch bark rolled along the ground. They all came to a stop against the side of a furry animal.

"Well, you two have certainly livened up our little forest," Sandy said. The birds and animals untangled themselves from each other. Nicholas and Edward tried to stand up. They were both a bit wobbly.

"Nicholas," Edward said, with an unsteady bow. "Here is the clue that I fought so hard to save for you."

"Edward, you were so brave to hold onto it against such a big bird. Thank you, my friend."

"Now," Sandy said, "take a look at the clue. It is what this entire hullabaloo has been about." Sandy gestured toward the bent and battered bark.

"Yes, the clue," Nicholas said. "Where did Francis go after Monadnock?" He gently unrolled the big piece of bark. The white outside had the black marks found on all birch bark.

With the help of the finches, who each stood on a corner, Nicholas looked at the tan inner bark side. The note was written in small mouse-sized letters. The badly damaged birch bark made it hard to read.

"Here, let me help you, Nicholas. The lettering is small but I can read it," Sandy said. Slowly she pieced together the words.

> Here is a note for you to see
> A stone wall divides a good neighbor from me
> Boyhood fun is found in a birch tree
> The house of a poet is where I will be

Nicholas followed Sandy's reading hopefully. When she finished, he sat back and sighed. "Stone walls, birch trees, that could be anywhere," Nicholas said. "That describes many places in New England."

"Don't forget the house of the poet," Edward said. "I fancy myself a bit of poet, you know. Let me see. Who is a poet from New Hampshire?" Edward paced back and forth with his front paws behind his back.

Sandy had hopped away a bit from the other animals. She was gazing at the stone wall mumbling to herself. In a moment, she came back. Edward was reciting bits of his own poetry, and the finches were discussing how to divide the state in their search.

"Quiet everyone, please be quiet. I believe I have figured it out," she said. Everyone stopped and looked at the hare. "I think I have figured out your cousin's clue. The part about the poet is the key. There are many poets and writers from New Hampshire. Why, this forest was once owned by a famous author."

"I see," Edward interrupted. "So you're saying Francis is somewhere in this forest?"

"No, no, please let me finish," Sandy said. "The poet part is the key, as I said. But the other lines helped me figure out the clue. Stone walls and birch trees are something Robert Frost knew about. He had a farm over in Derry. Francis must have gone to Robert Frost's house."

"Ah, yes, I was just coming to the same conclusion," Edward said. "Of course, Robert Frost wrote many poems about nature and New England and sleigh rides."

"Yes, well, Edward, we can talk about it as we travel," Nicholas said. "We need to catch up with Francis before he leaves Derry. I do wish I knew why he was on the run like this. How far away is Derry?" Nicholas asked Sandy.

"I have never been that far," Sandy said.

"We have been there," the finches piped up. They had been listening to all the talk about poets and writers. Travel was something they knew about. "We can carry you there in a day, I would say."

"I don't know about that," Edward said. "You seem a little small to take the two of us all the way."

"Well, if we each take a corner of the bark, I think we can manage it," the finch said. He looked to his three friends. They all nodded, wanting to help.

"It would be like a sleigh ride of our own," Nicholas said. Edward looked doubtful, but he didn't like the idea of walking all the way to Derry.

Nicholas and Edward scrambled onto the curled up birch bark. The four finches each grabbed a corner. They blew up a bit of dust and pine needles with their takeoff. "Good-bye and good luck," Sandy shouted over the noise.

Nicholas and Edward didn't dare wave back. They were trying to hold onto the swaying birch bark. "Good-bye, Sandy," Nicholas shouted over the edge of the bark. Edward kept his eyes closed and didn't say anything. He never did learn to like flying.

Chapter Eleven

They left the Shieling Forest and the town of Peterborough behind and headed east. They flew toward the rising sun. It inched up over the horizon in the still of the morning. They flew among the hills and mountains of southern New Hampshire.

Ahead, Nicholas saw a river snake its way down a valley heading south. He wanted to ask the finches what river it was, but he didn't want to interrupt their concentration. Edward didn't seem to be interested in his surroundings. Nicholas watched cars and trucks travel along a highway near the river.

Nicholas could see a city ahead. The river flowed along its edge. Rows of long brick buildings lined one side of the river. A tall tower jutted up into the sky. The finches swerved toward it. They were all out of breath.

The tower roof was clad in green copper. The glass in the round and ornate upper windows had broken long ago. The birds flew inside the open window. "We had to stop," the finch said. "This trip has taken longer than we thought." All four finches let go of the birch bark, and Nicholas and Edward tumbled onto the floor.

Edward sat up and watched the finches scatter around looking for some stray rainwater. "Are we in Derry?" he asked.

Nicholas got off the birch bark and sniffed around. "Where are we? This place kind of scares me." The finches, sipping water from a nearby puddle, looked up.

"We're in Manchester. It is one of the biggest cities in New Hampshire. This is part of the old Amoskeag mill works," the finch said.

Clouds started to fill in the sky. The sunny morning was gone. The wind through the open window was cold. Nicholas shivered. "I don't like the feeling of this place," he said.

Edward was coming around after his flight. "Oh, I don't know, Nicholas. This place has lots of character. Why, if we had time, I would like to look around a bit."

As Edward talked, a brick in the sidewall slid, creating an opening. A nose belonging to a gruff old rat sniffed through the opening.

"Who is that?" Nicholas asked. He pointed toward the opening and the rat nose. The rat popped out of the opening. A swarm of others followed. Rats filled the tower room. Their long bald tails swished back and forth. Their wiry whiskers brushed by Nicholas and Edward.

The finches flew off, twittering to themselves, and Nicholas froze in place. Edward stood beside him on the very tips of his little paws. The rats circled in closer and closer.

"What are you two doing in our mill?" one very husky rat asked. "There is nothing here for you," he said. The other rats murmured their agreement. "We control everything in this building," he added.

"We don't want anything," Nicholas said. "We stopped here accidentally."

"Now, see here," Edward managed to get out, "my friend and I mean no harm. We are merely resting. Now we will be on our way." Edward attempted to move, but the husky rat stopped him.

"Hold on there. Now that you're here, I have to take you to the big cheese rat. He will decide if you can stay or go."

"Now we really don't want to bother this 'Big Cheese'," Edward said. "I'm sure he is very busy."

"Yes," Nicholas added, "I think we should be on our

way. If you help us to call back our feathered friends, we won't bother you any more."

"Your friends have all gone," the rat said. "You'd better come with us now." The big rat led the way. The others stayed around Nicholas and Edward. They moved toward a trapdoor in the floor. Nicholas and Edward hesitated. The swarm of rats carried them along. Down the stairs they went. Down into the dark mill.

Chapter Twelve

The old mill smelled musty to Nicholas. It had started to rain outside and Nicholas could hear it drumming on the copper roof. Water dripped from cracks in the walls. The swarm of rats splashed through shallow puddles on the floor. Nicholas shivered as his paws hit the water. Edward paused at the edge of the puddle. The rats pushed him along.

"There is no need to shove," Edward said. "I just don't want to get my paws wet."

The rats snickered and kept them moving. They snaked their way through the cavernous room. The looms and bobbin machines stood silently in the dark. It looked like a dizzying maze to Nicholas. The rats knew where they were going.

Nicholas and Edward stayed close to each other. At first, they couldn't see anything in the dim light that filtered through a dusty window. Then, Nicholas noticed a rat sitting in the corner. It was looking toward them.

"Who are you?" the rat asked from the corner. "Why are you in my mill?"

"We didn't mean to stop here," Nicholas said. "We only wanted to rest a while."

"This is no place for a little mouse," the rat said. "Who is that with you?"

"This is my friend Edward. He is traveling with me."

"Now see here," Edward said. "We didn't mean to trespass in your mill. It certainly seems big enough for everyone."

"It is not for you to say what this mill should be for," the rat said.

"Maybe we should go along then," Nicholas said. "We don't want to come here and tell you about your own mill." Nicholas looked at his friend when he said this.

"These old buildings have been here for over one hundred years," the rat said. "They have seen many people come and go. We rats are the only ones who remain."

"Yes, well, there's not much to this mill now, is there?" Edward said. "I mean to say, it is just dead space."

"For many years these mills were the life of the city. The looms rumbled for hours and hours each day. Young women and children worked the clattering machines." The old rat moved out of the shadow in the corner and approached Nicholas and Edward.

"These mills were alive with the sound of thousands of workers. My family remembers the miles of cloth made here. We also remember the day this mill went dark." The rat reached out and touched Nicholas.

"It must have been a busy place," Nicholas said.

"Bells signaled the start of the day. The workers streamed into the building for work. Now it is always quiet. Now we sit in the dark and wait for the bells to toll again."

"It doesn't sound very healthy, sitting around in the dark and damp all the time," Edward said. "Now Nicholas and I, we are always on the move. Why, just today, we were flying with some finches over your city. Flying takes some getting used to," Edward added.

"You have flown with the birds?" the rat asked. "I have always wanted to fly. We live indoors all the time. What is it like?"

"You would love it," Nicholas said quickly. "You can feel the wind in your whiskers. There is so much to see. The excitement of taking off and landing is the best."

"Do you think I could fly?" the rat asked Nicholas. "I mean, could one of the birds carry me? I'll tell you what. If you help me to fly, I'll show you the way out of this mill."

Nicholas and Edward looked at each other. This was a very heavy rat. They didn't think the finches would be able to carry him. They didn't want to hurt his feelings. But they also needed to find their way out of the building.

"Now let me see," Edward said. "Flying is all about proper weight ratios and aerodynamics. I don't see how," Edward continued. The rat looked down with a sad face.

"I don't see how we can say no," Nicholas interrupted. "Let us go back up to the tower. I know we can get you flying."

"Do you think so? I have always imagined what it would be like to be a bird soaring in the air. They look so free," he ended.

Nicholas and Edward raced up the stairs and out to the bell tower. It had stopped raining but it was still gray and cold. A flock of pigeons huddled together for warmth in one corner.

Nicholas approached them and explained what he needed. Most of the birds ignored him and kept their eyes shut against the wind. One shaggy old pigeon, gray and purple, listened. "At least I will get out of this cold wind," he said.

They made their way into the building where the rat was waiting. "I knew you would come back," he said.

The gray pigeon introduced himself. "Hello there, I'm Gus. I understand you want to fly. I must say I've lived in Manchester all my life and I never saw a flying rat before."

"How do you do, Gus? I'm Rusty. I have never seen a pigeon that would fly with a rat before."

"I tell you what," Gus said. "I'll take you for a ride if your rats will gather up some old cotton from the mill for our pigeon nests. What do you say?"

"If you take me flying, you have a deal," Rusty said.

Nicholas and Edward looked at each other. If this pigeon could carry the gruff old rat, they could get out of the dark mill. They could continue their journey and catch up with Nicholas's cousin.

Chapter Thirteen

"Now, let's see about a flying lesson for Rusty," Nicholas said. Nicholas wanted to help Rusty to fly but he also wanted to get out of the mill. Edward remained silent, off to one side.

"I guess you can climb up on my back," Gus said. Rusty shuffled over and landed with an oomph on Gus's back.

"Easy does it, Rusty," Gus said. "Ok, here we go." Gus flapped his wings. His head bobbed back and forth, as he strutted along the floor. Rusty gripped him tightly and tried to see around the pigeon's head.

Gus lifted off and landed once, then twice. Rusty looked very nervous. They were getting close to a big loom. Nicholas and Edward watched. They ran after the bird. "Look out," Nicholas shouted.

"I don't think I want to fly," Rusty shouted.

"I think we are going to do it," Gus said and leapt off the ground. They were in the air. They just missed the top of the loom. "We did it," Gus shouted.

"I'm flying!" Rusty shouted with wild glee.

"You did it!" Nicholas shouted at the pair. He jumped up and down.

"Can we go now?" Edward asked.

Gus zoomed through the mill room. He soared high among the hanging lights. He wove among the looms. A huge grin spread across Rusty's whiskered face. Nicholas clapped his paws seeing the old rat smile.

Gus made his final turn, aimed for Nicholas and Edward, and skidded to a stop just short of a black puddle.

"That was more fun than I have had in years," Rusty said, jumping off the pigeon. "Did you see how we just missed hitting the lights?" he asked. "I never dreamed I could fly like that. I can see you and I are going to be great friends." Rusty ran up to the very tired pigeon.

"I tell you what," Gus said. "You lose a little weight and we'll try that again."

"I'm glad we could help you with your wish, Rusty," Nicholas said. "Edward and I have had a lot of help during our travels. We are happy to help someone else this time. Isn't that right, Edward?"

Edward had wandered away from the group. He turned around when he heard his name. "You know, Nicholas, we should really be on our way. Remember we were headed to Derry?"

"You helped me out," Rusty said. "Now I will help you out. It is not so easy, finding your way down out of this building, but I know a way."

"When I come back," he said to Gus, "we'll talk about the cotton for your nests."

Rusty turned and beckoned Nicholas and Edward to follow. He headed to a sidewall of the main room. "The stairs have been blocked for years. We'll follow the pipes inside the wall."

Gus led them to a rusty pipe sticking out of a hole in the wall. He jumped on and nimbly started down. Nicholas followed close behind. Edward seemed a bit hesitant. "Are you sure it's safe?" he asked.

"Edward, if a big rat like me can do it, you can, too," Gus said.

"It will be all right, Edward. Just stay behind me," Nicholas said.

"Of course I can do it," Edward said. "I just am concerned for our safety." He carefully crept onto the pipe. They were inside the walls of the mill now. The space was a maze of metal pipes and hanging wires. Cobwebs clung to everything. Edward shivered. "It is certainly drafty in here," he said.

Rusty never hesitated. He followed a well-established route. He jumped over gaps in the piping. He avoided the dangling wires and he brushed right through the cobwebs. Gus ducked into the end of a large pipe and Nicholas followed. When Edward reached the pipe, he stopped. Nicholas turned around.

"What's the matter, Edward? Why are you standing there?"

"Nothing's the matter," Edward said. "I just don't see that it is necessary to go through that dangerous-looking pipe."

"It's not dangerous. See, Rusty has gone through, and now I am in the pipe."

"That's just it. I'm not sure the pipe will hold all three of us," Edward said.

Nicholas could see his friend was nervous about the dark, enclosed spaces. "Edward, if a little mouse like me can get through safely, I'm sure you can, too. After all, think about all the brave things you have done." Nicholas backed into the pipe.

"Yes, that's right," Edward said. "I did fight a pack of weasels once." He stepped into the opening. "Don't forget the time I got us onto a train in Massachusetts." Edward was jogging along now, trying to catch up to Nicholas. "I have done so many brave things," he was saying as he ran out of the pipe and into the morning light.

"You did it," Nicholas said to his friend. The pipe opened up on the outside of the building. They were standing on a narrow ledge next to the river.

"Thank you, my friend," Edward said to Nicholas. He knew he would not have made it through the pipe without his friend's help.

"Just follow the Merrimac River for a while," Gus was saying. "Then, head east. It will take you right to Derry. It's not far."

The two friends followed the granite ledge along the river. The rain had stopped and the sun was out. Nicholas hoped he would catch up with his cousin soon.

Chapter Fourteen

Nicholas and Edward walked along quietly. It was late in the year but the sunshine felt warm after the gloom and damp of the old mill. They listened to the sound of the Merrimac River smoothly flowing south. The water moved faster than they could walk. They watched a tree branch drift by on the water.

"Think how nice it would be to travel on the river," Nicholas said. "We could just sit in the sun and make progress without having to do anything."

"Now that sounds good to me," Edward said. "I didn't like be out on the ocean in a fishing boat but this river seems tame enough." The two animals chuckled over the memory of their adventure on a Gloucester fishing boat. A cold wind blew across the water.

"Come on, Nicholas, let's get moving or we'll never make it to Derry."

They traveled away from the river. They scrambled through patches of woods, along hedges, and through backyards. They started across the lawn of one run-down house. The uncut grass hid them from view of the windows. They paused for a breath next to a rotting stack of firewood.

"If we can get through this yard, it looks like there are no more houses for a while," Nicholas said. They both knew that humans don't always like to see small animals running through their yards.

"Are you ready for the last dash?" Nicholas asked. Both animals started out sprinting. As soon as they cleared the woodpile, they heard "woof, woof, woof" coming from the house. "A dog," Nicholas shouted. He didn't care for dogs. They could be as much trouble as a cat to a little mouse. Edward didn't like trouble of any kind. Both animals took off at a run.

"Head for the woods," Edward shouted. They hadn't gotten very far when a black-and-white spotted dog bounded up. He got between the animals and the trees. The dog knelt down and sniffed. He barked, wagged his tail, and bounced at the frightened animals.

"Hey, where you guys going?" the dog asked. "I don't get many visitors out this way." The dog panted with his tongue hanging out of his mouth. A long drop of saliva landed very close to Edward. "Say, what's your name?" the dog asked.

"Now see here. There's no need to bother about us," Edward said. "We are just passing through. We don't mean any harm to you."

"Why would you harm me?" the dog asked. "I didn't do anything. Hey, you guys want to come see my collection of old shoes. I have shoes from all over the neighborhood." The dog jumped in the direction of his house.

"My, that sounds fascinating, but we really need to press on," Edward said.

"Doesn't it?" the dog said. "Come on, just watch out for the cat. He scratches," the dog ended in a whisper.

"Really," Nicholas said, "my friend and I need to keep moving. We want to be in Derry by the time it gets dark."

The dog said, "How about we chase a few squirrels? They like to come down from the trees this time of day. Usually this is my nap time." The dog ran off toward a tree, barking loudly. Neither Nicholas nor Edward could see a squirrel anywhere.

The dog ran back and sat. He scratched away at his side with his hind leg. "I sure get itchy sometimes, you know what I mean?"

"I'm sure we don't," Edward said. "Well, it was very pleasant to meet you."

The dog stood up. "Hey, I didn't tell you my name. I'm Zeke, but sometimes around here, they call me 'that dang dog.' Kind of a funny name, isn't it? You can call me Zeke."

"It is nice to meet you, Zeke," Nicholas said. "But, we really do need to find our way to Derry." Edward started moving toward the woods. Nicholas followed him. Zeke sagged down to the ground.

"That's all right. I have lots of things I have to do anyway," Zeke said. "I guess you guys have important things to do. Maybe I'll see you when you come back this way?"

Nicholas turned around and looked into the saddest pair of brown eyes he had ever seen. Edward was still walking forward. "Well, I guess it would only be polite to stay a little while. What do you think, Edward?"

Zeke didn't wait to hear what Edward thought. He bounded after the two small animals. He circled them, slowly drawing them back toward his yard. "What do you want to do first? Do you want to dig for a bone or something? I know I have a bunch buried out here somewhere."

"Now, now, Zeke, do be careful," Edward said. "There is no need to step on us." Zeke surged ahead, leading Nicholas toward the house.

"I'll be careful. I'll be careful. We'll have fun. You'll see," Zeke said.

Edward could see this stop might take a while. He shrugged and followed Nicholas and Zeke toward the old rundown house.

Chapter Fifteen

Zeke raced ahead of Nicholas and Edward. The house was of the classic New England style. There was a big house, a little house, a back house, and a barn all attached to each other. At one time, the structure must have been white. Now, the cedar clapboards and trim boards were just weathered wood. Smoke curled out of the chimney of the little house.

"Come on. We can play in the barn, if you want. There's always something fun to do in the barn."

"We are very tired from our long day," Edward said. "Perhaps we can just get something to eat and go to sleep."

"I think Edward is right. We have had a very long day. Maybe we can play tomorrow?"

"You have to come in the house," Zeke said. "I bet we can find something to eat." The dog led the way through the doors of the connecting buildings from the barn into the house. Inside, a shaded light sat on the kitchen table. The woodstove radiated heat. Zeke's toenails clicked on the old linoleum floor.

"There you are, old boy," a woman said to the dog. Nicholas and Edward scrambled away into the deep shadows. "Come here, old fella," she said again. "Sit next to me. The woman groaned as she sat down in a creaky rocker by the woodstove.

"Tell me now, what have you been up to, old fella?" Zeke sat next to the woman and let her rough up his head with her weathered hand.

"Doesn't that feel nice, hey boy? You listen to what I have been working on all day. Then, I'll get you some dinner." The woman rocked in her chair. In a singsong voice, she began to recite lines of a long poem. It was about the history of New Hampshire. Zeke had heard many versions of it before.

She spoke of granite, farmers, fishermen, and patriots. There was a president named Pierce, an old man of the mountain, and a Concord coach. She included Sarah Josepha Hale and a little lamb's tale. So many people, so many things were in the poem Zeke could never keep it all straight. He knew she would go on for a while in her steady low voice. Slowly, Zeke crept away to look for Nicholas and Edward.

He found them in the back house next to the barn. It was cold out here, away from the woodstove. Their breath came out in little puffs of steam.

"I say, we should go now," Edward was saying. "We still have a long way to travel and we have no idea if Francis is even in Derry."

"I know, but I think we should at least spend the night with Zeke. He seems kind of lonely," Nicholas said. "We can leave for Derry tomorrow."

"Hey, you guys weren't going to leave, were you?" Zeke said as he came into the room. "Soon, she'll fall asleep in her chair. You can come in and have some of my dinner." Nicholas and Edward looked at each other. They followed Zeke back into the kitchen.

The woman had set out Zeke's dish next to the stove. Nicholas and Edward had been traveling for a long time. They were used to making meals wherever they could find them. The mouse and chipmunk were not going to turn down dried dog food if that's all there was to eat.

Zeke buried his face in his bowl. Nicholas and Edward each held a piece of dried food. It was quiet except for the sound of chewing and the crackling of wood in the fire.

"I know what we'll do," the woman shouted and

awoke out of her chair. Zeke jumped, but did not stop eating. Nicholas and Edward threw down their food and hid under the table. "Zeke, tomorrow you and I are going over to the Frost place. It always gives me inspiration for my poetry when I hike around that old property."

The woman paced around her kitchen. "We'll take the Franklin. It will do it some good to get it out on the road. What do you say, Zeke?"

Zeke looked up. He thought to himself. He was about to go back to eating when he noticed Nicholas and Edward. They were listening from behind the wide turned leg of the kitchen table. That was it! His new friends needed to get to Derry, to Robert Frost's place. Now, here was his chance to help them.

"Do you want to take a ride over to Derry tomorrow?" the woman asked again. Zeke barked loudly. "Sure you do," she said. "We'll drive over there tomorrow." She tousled Zeke's head one more time and tottered off to bed.

Zeke was happy. He circled his bed near the woodstove. He liked riding in the antique car over the back roads. Tomorrow he would spend more time with his new friends. They could romp through the woods all day. The woman would follow behind speaking her lines of poetry to herself. Maybe they would stop for burgers on the way home. All he had to do was make sure he got them to the car in time.

Chapter Sixteen

Nicholas and Edward slept in the barn. They stayed up in the loft, buried among last year's hay. A cast-iron hook, used to lift hay bales to the loft, swung on a rope in a light breeze. All else was still.

Edward tossed and turned. He worried about missing their ride. He was getting tired of the chase after Francis. He wanted to find Nicholas's cousin. He wanted to help his friend find the journal. Then he wanted to go home. When Edward finally fell asleep, he dreamed of returning to the pine forests and cranberry bogs of Massachusetts.

Edward awoke suddenly with the feeling that he was being watched. He laid dead still, the way a wild animal can, and scanned the dark barn. Nicholas continued to sleep nearby. Sitting on a beam overhead, Edward noticed an owl. Like him, the owl did not move. He could not tell if the owl saw them covered up in the hay.

Nicholas twitched in his sleep. The owl swiveled his head toward the noise. Edward gasped. The owl had found them. He whispered to his friend.

"Nicholas, wake up. We have to get out of here."

Nicholas rolled over and opened his eyes. "What is it, Edward? Is it morning already?"

"No, now be quiet, Nicholas. There is a barn owl watching us. We have to find a way out of here before he gets us."

Nicholas was wide-awake now. The two animals burrowed down in the hay. The owl swooped down and grasped at the spot they had just left. The owl snapped his beak in frustration. Edward chattered excitedly and Nicholas squeaked as they ran along the wall. The owl fluttered back up to the beam.

The sky was lightening up. They could hear noises coming from the house. "Zeke must be up," Edward said. "We have to get down to the car. Somehow, we need to distract the owl."

"You can't hide from me for long," they heard the owl say. "This is my barn. I will find you soon enough." He flapped his wings and flew around in a circle high in the barn.

Edward and Nicholas hid beneath a brace in the wall. They could hear the old woman in the house. She rattled around in the kitchen. Zeke paced back and forth following her. "Come now, Zeke," they heard her say. "I'll pack us a lunch, then we'll be off."

"We don't have much time," Nicholas said. "How are we going to get away from this owl? I can't see where he is now."

The big bird sat still watching for the animals. He waited patiently for them. He knew, in time, they had to come out.

At a sound from below, the owl flew at the little mouse at once. The owl's talons thumped into the old boards of the loft. He had just missed! Nicholas scampered back as fast as he could. His heart beat rapidly.

"We will have to split up. You go in one direction, and I will go in another," Edward said. "The owl can't chase us both at the same time."

"What if he catches you?" Nicholas said. "I can't let him harm you, Edward."

"Nonsense, Nicholas, I'll dodge and weave so fast he won't be able to follow me." Edward sounded brave, but Nicholas could see his friend was nervous. "It is the only way we will get out of here," Edward added. "When I count to three, we will go. One, two, three!" Edward said. He made a dash for the ladder leading down to the ground.

Nicholas ran in the opposite direction. He didn't have time to think. The owl screeched and swooped after Edward. Nicholas ran for the edge of the loft. He heard a scream that could only be his friend. He looked back as he ran. Edward was in the owl's talons.

The owl flew low over the loft. He swerved around the iron hook. Nicholas, watching in horror, ran after the bird and his friend. Nicholas leaped out over the edge of the loft for the iron hook. His little paws grabbed the rope. With one big swoop, the whole thing swung in a great arc.

Nicholas and the iron hook connected with the bird. The owl lost its grip on Edward. Edward reached for the hook. With Nicholas and Edward together on the hook, it started to plunge down to the ground. They screamed as it picked up speed.

Zeke had been running back and forth from the barn to the house. He followed the old woman as she lugged a lunch basket. She folded back the soft top of the antique car. She opened the driver's side door and whistled for Zeke to hop up. She started the engine. As she pulled away, the hook clunked down in the back.

Nicholas and Edward landed in the picnic basket on top of a loaf of bread. The hook bounced out. Zeke stuck his head over the seat. "Hey, are you two coming to Derry with us?" Edward and Nicholas collapsed into the basket. They watched the owl fly out through the barn door, headed for the forest and an easier breakfast.

Chapter Seventeen

Nicholas and Edward sat quietly in the picnic basket for the short ride to Derry. The old lady drove slowly down back roads. In the pale blue sky, the wintery sun flickered through the bare trees. Tall brown grass, frosted white with the morning cold, lined both sides of the road.

Zeke looked out the side window. They pulled into an old farm just like the one he lived on. The old woman stopped in a small dirt parking area behind the barn. When she let him out, Zeke ran over to a stone wall running back into the woods along one side of an old meadow. Small birch trees leaned over the wall from the forest side.

While the old lady was busy, Nicholas and Edward hopped out of the basket and hid behind the back tire. "This must be Robert Frost's place. Francis must be here somewhere," Nicholas said. "I bet he's up in the barn there. That is just the kind of place a mouse would want to live."

"Let's wait for the old lady to leave before we go look," Edward said. "I don't think I can take any more excitement today. I hope Francis is still here."

Zeke came back and sniffed around the basket. "Let's go for a walk first, Zeke. Then we'll come back and have lunch." Zeke wasn't listening. The old lady headed for an opening in the stone wall that led out to the woods.

"Hey, what are you guys doing here?" Zeke asked when he saw the two animals hiding behind the tire.

"We needed a ride to Derry, remember Zeke?" Nicholas said. "We're looking for my cousin Francis. He should be here somewhere."

"I hope so," Edward said. "We've been chasing after him for a long time now. Zeke bounded off, not really listening anymore. He was hot on the trail of something really smelly. The old woman was off on her jaunt. She spoke aloud lines of her poem as she walked. Edward and Nicholas trudged up the grassy slope to the barn.

Everything was closed up tight for the winter. However, small animals, like Nicholas and Edward, can always find a way. Once inside, Nicholas ran ahead shouting for his cousin. Edward squeezed through the same small opening and waited near the wall. "Francis, are you here?" Nicholas shouted in his high mouse voice.

Nicholas made his way through the building. His voice grew fainter. Edward could just hear him calling out, "Francis, it's me, your cousin Nicholas." He thought he would let Nicholas look around for himself for a while. Edward found a sunny spot near the window and curled up for a little mid-morning nap.

Nicholas found himself in the big house part of the building. He walked around the old furniture, looking for signs of his cousin. He noticed a dish on the floor with some cat food still in it. A bowl next to it held water. He sipped the water. It was cold and tasted fresh.

Nicholas knew enough about cats to know that, where there was a cat, probably there weren't any mice. Nicholas suddenly felt very sad. He might have misread the clue. Francis could be long gone. To be sure, he thought he'd better look in all the rooms.

He made his way upstairs to the small bedrooms. He pushed open the door of one room. He thought he heard a familiar squeak. He stood still listening. His whiskers quivered. He tried to sense what was in the room.

"Francis," Nicholas whispered. He remembered there might be a cat in the house. "Francis, are you here?" He peeked around the edge of the thin door. From under a bed poked a whiskered nose. It looked like Nicholas's nose. It sniffed at the air the same way Nicholas did.

"Who's there?" the mouse under the bed said.

"It's me, Nicholas. Is that you, Francis?" Nicholas rushed up to the bed and lifted the overhanging spread. A small brown mouse stared back at Nicholas.

"What are you doing wandering around in the daylight? Have you seen Tabby?"

"Francis?" Nicholas asked. Just as the other mouse was about to speak, a fluffed up, orange-striped cat meowed fiercely. It was right behind the mice. They both shrieked and ran under the bed. The tabby wedged itself under the bed, following the pair.

"Come with me," the little mouse said. "I've told you not to be wandering around during the day. Tabby never misses a thing." The mice ran along the baseboard, around the room, and out the door. Tabby popped out from under the bed. She skidded across the wood floor and bumped into the door. It closed, locking her inside.

The two mice ran down the stairs and out through the kitchen to the barn. Edward, sleeping in the sun, heard them and hopped up. He rubbed his eyes and looked first at Nicholas and then at the second mouse. "Nicholas, you found your cousin," he said.

Chapter Eighteen

"Are you Francis?" Nicholas asked.

Edward looked from one mouse to the other. In the dim light, Edward thought the two mice looked like each other. "I believe we have found your cousin, Nicholas."

"Why are you looking for Francis?" the mouse said. "Who are you? How did you hear what happened?"

Nicholas looked at Edward. The mouse's questions puzzled the two animals. "What are you talking about? Aren't you Francis?" Nicholas asked quietly.

"Francis was here, but I missed him," the mouse said. "I'm Sam. I followed Francis from Maine. He was so upset when he left. I wanted to catch up with him. Did you find his clues, too?"

"You're not Francis?" Edward said.

"Francis is my brother. We live in Maine. He is the one interested in our family history."

"Where is he?" Nicholas asked. "Edward and I have been trying to catch up with him. I thought he was in Maine, and then we followed him to New Hampshire."

"I don't know where he is," Sam said. "When I heard a mouse in the house I thought it might be him."

"What about the clues? Didn't he leave a clue about where he went? Why didn't he just tell you where he was going?"

"Francis didn't want anyone to find out about the journal."

"You have seen the journal?" Nicholas said. "That's why we have been looking for Francis. My family's copy was ruined. We heard Francis had the only other copy."

"Francis has it still," Sam said. He looked away, twitching his nose. "Francis would spend hours reading it. He loved all the old stories."

"Francis has the journal?" Nicholas said. He was getting nervous now. "I have come so far. I have been away from my family for a very long time."

"We have traveled for a long time," Edward said. "I have helped you for months and months. Don't forget, I found out Francis was in New Hampshire while you were looking for him in Maine."

"That's right," Nicholas said. "Edward and I have

traveled all over New England together looking for my family journal. I would have been in trouble many times over without Edward."

"Tell us," Edward said. "What happened to the journal?"

"Well, nothing has happened to it, as far as I know. If you can catch up with Francis, maybe he can tell you," Sam said.

"When Francis first read the journal, he was so excited about our family history he wanted to share it with everyone. Then, one day, he just changed," Sam said. "One day he was reading from it and laughing at something. The next day he wouldn't talk about it any more. He just jumped up and said he had found it."

"What?" Nicholas shouted. "What did he find in the journal? It is just a collection of all our family stories. What did he read in the journal?"

"Francis wouldn't tell me," Sam said. "He kept it very secret. When he first got the journal, he was always telling me stories from it. After a while, whenever I asked him about it, he wouldn't say anything. He told me I wouldn't be interested in those old stories."

"Now see here, Sam," Edward said. "We have been after that journal for a long time. You have got to tell us what you know."

Sam looked at Nicholas and Edward for a moment. "All I know," Sam eventually said, "was that the journal held some secret. After that, he wouldn't tell me any more. He just left. I found a note that told me to look for clues. It said not to tell anyone, and Francis would explain everything if I could catch up with him."

"I followed him here using the clues. I have been searching everywhere for the next clue, but I can't find it anywhere," Sam said.

Nicholas just sat in the dark barn without speaking. This whole search for the journal might end right here. Francis had taken it somewhere, and Nicholas and Edward couldn't find him. Nicholas looked over at Edward, who was looking out the window. "I don't blame you if you want to just go home now," Nicholas said to his friend.

"But I still need to find my brother," Sam said. "I need to get him to come home. I need to help him if I can."

A small smile broke out on Edward's face. As Edward watched, Zeke came bounding out of the woods. He trotted along, his head high with something held tightly in his mouth. Zeke sat down under a single gnarled apple tree in the meadow behind the barn.

"What has that silly dog found?" Edward said, mostly to himself.

The three animals made their way over to the tree. None of them wanted to talk about the journal right now. Zeke ran up to them. "Hey, where did you guys come from? Did you follow me here from my house?"

"Zeke, don't you remember? We came over here in the old car with you," Edward said.

"Oh, that's right, that's right, sometime I forget things," Zeke said. "Hey, guess what I found out in the woods by the stone wall? You'll never guess."

They looked at the curious wooden object Zeke had dropped in front of them. Mice teeth had gnawed and given it shape. "It looks like a boat," Nicholas said. "It looks like a mouse has made this." He turned it over. On the back, written in small mouse-style writing, was the name Francis.

Chapter Nineteen

"It looks like a boat," Nicholas said again. "Francis must have made this as a clue. But what does it mean?"

"I have searched this property everywhere and never saw this," Sam said. "Where did you find it?" He looked at Zeke, who smiled with a silly grin.

"I was lying right there on the ground," Zeke said. "All I had to do was dig around a stone that had fallen off the wall. There it was, underneath the stone."

"That's all you had to do?" Edward said. "No wonder you didn't find it, Sam. That stone must have fallen on the boat and covered it up."

"But what kind of clue is it?" Nicholas asked. "Do you think Francis was trying to float away down the brook?"

"Nicholas, it is much too small for that," Edward said. "He must have wanted us to know he was going to where boats are used."

"Francis doesn't like the water very much," Sam said. "If he was headed for the water, he must have a good reason. He has been heading west all the time."

"I bet he's going to the ocean," Nicholas said suddenly. "I bet he is going back to Uncle William's place, down on Martha's Vineyard, with the journal."

"Now, Nicholas," Edward said. "If Francis was going there, I don't think he would go by boat."

"That's right," Sam said. "Maybe he is going to Lake Winnipesaukee. It's the biggest lake in the state. If he wants to hide out, there are many inlets and islands on the lake. He would need a boat there for sure."

"I think you might be right," Edward said. "After all, I heard long ago he was somewhere in the White Mountains. Winnipesaukee is near the mountains. He must have gone there."

Nicholas looked from Sam to Edward. He was tired and he didn't want to argue with his friend. If they were right, Nicholas would have to travel north many miles. It was the beginning of winter. Snow would be falling soon. He wanted to be right. He wanted to spend the winter somewhere warm and safe.

"I believe Francis is headed south to the ocean," Nicholas said firmly. "I think we should head that way right away, before it snows."

"Nicholas, you heard Sam. He thinks Francis is heading west. He wouldn't be going back to the ocean."

"I am going that way because I believe Francis went that way," Nicholas said. Edward looked at his old friend. He could see he wouldn't be able to change his mind.

"If you think Francis is going to the ocean, then you should look for him there," Edward said. "I am going north. Remember, my aunt and uncle live in the White Mountains, Nicholas. If you don't find Francis, you can look for me there."

Nicholas didn't know what to say. He wasn't so sure about where Francis was now. He wanted to travel with Edward, but he wanted to be right, too. Sam was watching him. Zeke sat with the carved boat between his front paws. He picked up his ears.

"Come here, you old dog," they all heard coming from the edge of the woods. The old woman had come

back to her car. She whistled for Zeke. He bounced away but came back to the apple tree. "I have to go now. Can I take this stick with me?" he asked.

"You can take it. Can you give me a ride?" Nicholas asked the dog. "I will stay with you, then head south in the morning." Nicholas didn't want to look at Edward.

"Sure you can." Zeke let Nicholas scramble up to his collar. Nicholas held on to the black-and-white fur. Zeke picked up the stick and headed for the car.

"Good-bye, Nicholas," Edward called. "Look for me at Winnipesaukee."

Nicholas held on to Zeke's collar as he trotted off to the car. The old woman was packing her picnic basket. Nicholas jumped off Zeke's back and climbed into the back of the car. Zeke hopped into the front. In the car now, the old woman backed the car out of the parking lot.

Nicholas could see Edward and Sam sitting under the lone apple tree. The last of the dried leaves fluttered to the ground. His friend waved. Nicholas was not sure when he would see his friend again.

The car jogged down the rode. Alone in the back, Nicholas realized he had no idea where Edward's family lived. How was he going to find his friend again if he couldn't find Francis? The ride back to the farm was dark, cold, and very unhappy for Nicholas. He was not sure he had taken the right road back there at the Frost place.

Chapter Twenty

Back at the farmhouse, Nicholas stayed awake late into the night. From where he lay, he looked up at a map of New Hampshire framed on the kitchen wall. Nicholas could see that the coast was only a small portion of the state. If Francis were on the coast, it wouldn't take long to find him. Then he could catch up with Edward.

It was cold in the kitchen in the early morning. The woodstove had cooled off. There was a skim of thin ice in Zeke's water dish. "Good-bye, Zeke," Nicholas said. "Thank you for helping me. I wish I could stay longer, but I have to find my cousin." Nicholas shivered in the cold.

Zeke yawned deeply. "What's that now, Nicholas? Are you leaving?"

"I have to leave. I have to catch up with my cousin."

Zeke slurped Nicholas in the only way he could think of to say good-bye. Nicholas rubbed his face with his paws. "Thanks a lot, Zeke, good-bye."

Nicholas ran out of the house fast. He was sad and lonely and he missed his friend Edward already. He didn't know how he would find his cousin down on the coast but he had to try, with or without Edward. Nicholas, keeping the map from the kitchen in his mind, headed south toward the ocean.

He wandered along for miles on his own. He had learned long ago to use the sun to help him stay on course. The little mouse traveled in rugged thistle grass beside the road. He wandered among bare trees. He passed through small towns. Each night he slept in a hollow log, or an empty barn, or once, in an upside-down canoe.

One morning, he came to a river winding its way east. A busy road crossed the river on a green, high-arched bridge. Nicholas could see buildings clustered along the shore. A ship traveled slowly up the river.

Trucks growled and belched smoke on the roads.

"It is quite a sight," Nicholas heard a voice call out. "We come down to Portsmouth every winter," a small duck was saying. "Lot more action, a lot more noise. We kind of like it, for a while."

"Breaks up the routine up north," another duck said.

"Things get cold where we come from this time of year," a third duck said.

The raft of black-and-white ducks, floating in the cold river water, paddled against the strong current. "Do you live around here?" Nicholas asked. "Do you know any mice perhaps? I'm looking for my cousin. I think he might be here on the coast."

"Sure, we've seen mice," one duck said.

"Mostly down the river a ways," another said.

"There are old houses, and gardens, and barns," a third duck added. "There are all kinds of places for a mouse to live and find a meal," the first duck said.

"That sounds like something my cousin would enjoy. He likes to hear old stories and learn about history. How far away is it?" Nicholas tried to look from one duck to the next as they spoke.

"Not so far, we'll take you there," a duck said. The raft of five ducks moved in close to the bank. They liked to travel as a group. The lead duck let Nicholas climb onto his back. They shoved off and flowed downstream in the current.

As they floated, they told Nicholas about their home up in Canada. The buffleheads had traveled together for many years. They laughed at old jokes all the time. They told stories of their many trips together. Nicholas did his best to learn their names. They were Ethel, Fran, Burt, Stanley, and the youngest Kyle.

Nicholas tried to tell them about his travels. The ducks paddled under an old drawbridge and past oil storage tanks. They listened politely to Nicholas but started up talking again as soon as they could.

"So, then Stanley had to chip Burt out of the ice with his beak," Fran was finishing a story. All the other buffleheads laughed. They were approaching the south bank, past the city. They stopped near a collection of old homes. "This is Strawbery Banke," Fran was saying. "It is one of the oldest parts of Portsmouth. Some of these buildings were built before your American Revolution," Ethel added.

"Have a look around," Burt said. "There's a barn up the hill, ask for a horse named Betty. She'll know if your cousin is here."

"Yes, Betty draws a cart through the old town. She watches everything and everyone," Stanley said.

Nicholas jumped ashore. The ducks paddled off, getting ready to take flight. "Where are you going?" Nicholas asked.

"We're off to the Isle of Shoals, offshore a bit from here," Burt said. "No place for a mouse like you," Stanley said.

"I wouldn't venture offshore if I were you," Kyle said. "No mouse wants to bob around in a boat if they can stay safe on shore," Ethel said. "At least none I've ever heard of."

Nicholas waved good-bye. He wondered if Francis was the kind of mouse who would venture out on the ocean. He decided to find Betty and see if she had seen his cousin on the coast.

Chapter Twenty-One

The collection of old buildings known as Strawbery Banke sat around a big green lawn near the river. Each house had a garden, carefully protected against the coming winter. Nicholas searched out a meal among the dried plants still in the ground. As he sat eating, he heard a horse clomping along the path.

A bay-colored horse, covered in a red-and-green plaid blanket, pulled an empty wagon. As the horse passed, Nicholas dropped his meal and ran along beside the horse. "Excuse me, is your name Betty?"

The horse was startled. She missed her step and jostled the wagon. The driver clicked his tongue and flipped the reins to settle the horse.

"Be careful, little mouse. I don't want to roll over you with this big wagon," the horse said with a sigh. She plodded along at a steady pace. Nicholas ran beside the horse.

"Are you Betty?" Nicholas asked again. "Some friends told me you might have seen my cousin Francis."

"Yes, I'm Betty. There aren't too many mice around here this time of year, though. Mice like to stay warm and dry. Of course, I just see the same view all the time. When I'm not standing in the barn, I'm pulling this wagon around the grounds."

"I've been looking for my cousin and I think he might be down here near the ocean."

Betty shook her head up and down a bit. She sneezed. "Doesn't sound like a place a mouse would like to me," she said.

Nicholas was getting worried. Maybe he had been wrong about Francis. Maybe he wasn't at the ocean at all. Instead of getting closer to Francis, he was getting farther away from him all the time. He should have trusted Edward.

"I think I have made a mistake," Nicholas said to the horse. "I have to go north as fast as I can. I have to catch up with my friend Edward."

"Where is Edward now?" Betty asked. "Gee, I wish I could go with you. I sure could use a chance to stretch my legs. I haven't had a run for a long time."

"Why don't you come with me?" Nicholas asked. "There are a lot of back roads and paths in this state. You could run for as long as you wanted."

"Oh, I don't know. I'm kind of used to this path now," Betty said. "Besides, the driver is always around and he locks the barn every night."

"Edward has gone to Winnipesaukee. It is a big lake near the White Mountains," Nicholas said.

"Lakes, mountains, it all sounds wonderful," Betty said. "I'm tired of living in the city. Come to my barn tonight. If you help me get out, I'll carry you north," Betty decided suddenly. "Oh, this is so exciting. Imagine me, galloping through the night."

Nicholas spent the rest of the day sleeping under a mustard-yellow house. He wanted to be ready for a long ride through the night. As the sun set, he followed Betty into her barn. The driver rubbed down the horse, gave her some oats, and filled the big trough with water.

When he left the barn, the driver flipped a bar down, holding the door shut from the outside. It was a big piece of wood that pivoted at one end and fit into a notch on the door. From the ground, Nicholas could see it would be impossible to swing that up and open the door for Betty.

"How am I going to get Betty out?" he asked himself. Nicholas ducked back under the door and found Betty in her stall eating her dinner. She slowly munched the oats and thought about running through the long dark night.

"Betty, I don't think I can open the door for you," Nicholas said. "I don't see how we can get you out of this barn."

"But I have to get out. Have you looked at all the doors? There is a big sliding door in the back of the barn that is hardly ever used."

Nicholas ran down the length of the building to look. The door hung on a track. There was a small metal hook on the inside holding it closed. Nicholas thought this looked more manageable. He ran back to work out a plan with Betty, but when he got to her stall, it was empty.

"Betty, where are you?" Nicholas called out. The barn was quiet. He hadn't been gone very long. He heard noises out front. He noticed the barn door was open again. The driver was back.

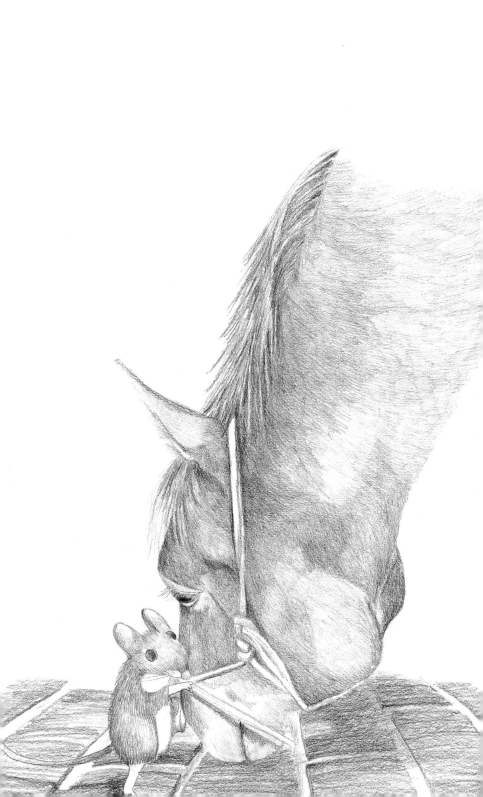

He was getting ready to hitch Betty to the wagon again. He wrapped a leading line from Betty's rope halter around a pole and went back in the barn.

"What's going on, Betty? What are you doing out here?" Nicholas asked.

"Sometimes I have to take people for rides around the city after dark," Betty said. "I guess I won't be able to go with you after all."

"No, you have to come with me now. I won't leave without you. What if we can get you unhooked?" Nicholas ran up to the pole and tried to gnaw through the halter. It was old rope and stiff in the cold. He didn't know how much time he would have to work before the driver came back.

Betty tugged on the line, which only made it tighter. "Hold still, Betty. I think I am getting it." They heard the driver inside rummaging around, looking for something.

"I don't think we have much time," Betty said.

Nicholas worked hard. He nipped the rope, yarn by yarn.

"Hey, what's going on out here?" The driver was outside now. "What are you doing, little mouse?" As Nicholas gnawed through the last bit of rope, Betty backed away. She lowered her head to let Nicholas climb up and hold onto her mane.

"Come on, let's go," he said. Betty neighed happily and brushed past the driver. She broke into a gallop and was quickly out of sight in the dark. The driver sat down on a bench, scratching his head. He wasn't sure what had just happened. He didn't know what he would say the next day if Betty didn't come back.

Chapter Twenty-Two

Betty, with Nicholas clinging to her mane, ran on through the night. She couldn't remember when she had been this happy. Her mane flowed back in the wind. Her hooves pounded on the ground in a rhythm she hadn't heard in a long time. Every muscle in her body worked driving them on.

Nicholas was happy, too. He had been wrong about looking for his cousin near the coast. He should have listened to Edward. With the help of Betty, he would catch up with Edward and they would find his cousin.

They followed old roads through the woods. They rested at the edge of fields and slept under cover of trees. They talked with animals they met along the way. A gray catbird, flying south for the winter, stopped and gave them directions. They traveled north and west, away from the coast.

The hills grew higher and the air colder. In time, they approached the lake. Betty came to the top of a hill. The view opened out in front of them. Nicholas looked down into a valley. A lake, indented with coves and dotted with islands, spread out before them. Mountains protecting the northern shore marched into the distance.

"We made it, Nicholas. That was the best run I've had in my whole life," Betty said. She was happy, but tired. The two animals stood still looking out at the view. "So you think Francis is somewhere on this lake?" Betty asked. "How are you going to find him?"

"First, I have to catch up with Edward. When we are together, we can figure out a way to find Francis." Betty pawed at the ground with her hoof. She shivered with cold. Nicholas jumped down from the horse and landed among the pine needles.

"I will ask animals around here. Everyone always knows when Edward has been around," Nicholas said.

"I have been thinking," Betty said. "Maybe I should return to Portsmouth and my barn. The deep woods are no place for a horse like me. I've had a great run. It has been the run of a lifetime, but I do miss my stall and warm hay. Besides, I don't want my driver to get in trouble for letting me run away."

"You can go if you want to, Betty," Nicholas said. "I'll find Edward. I know it. I couldn't have made it this far without you. Thank you."

Nicholas watched Betty trot away down the hill. It was quiet here in the woods. Many animals had already burrowed in for the winter. Snow began to fall around him. The big flakes pattered on the dried leaves. Soon the snow had coated everything white. Nicholas shrugged the flakes off his fur and made his way toward the lake.

Summer cottages faced the western shore of the lake. Nicholas spent a few days going from camp to camp, looking for Edward. His friend, he knew, liked to stay warm and dry. Every place he stopped was quiet and empty. Nicholas was starting to feel as though he had made a mistake coming to the lake so late in the year.

He found a warm place to sleep inside a boathouse built right out over the water. A glossy wooden power-boat hung above the water stored for the winter. The cushioned seats made a snug nest. It grew dark quickly now and Nicholas spent much of his time dozing. He awoke late one night to a most eerie sound.

"Haoo, haoooo," went the voice. It was a strange laughing call. Nicholas wanted to find out who was making that odd sound. He climbed down from the boat and peeked out the window overlooking the water.

The lake, dotted with reflected starlight, was still. A nearby island, ringed with tall pines, broke up the view of the water. Between the island and the boathouse, Nicholas noticed a large bird standing up on the water flapping its wings. He heard the call again. "Haoo, Haoooo," went the bird.

From the shore of the island, Nicholas heard a voice carried over the still water. "Yes, yes, I am sorry to bother you so late. I am still looking for Francis." Nicholas recognized the voice right away. It was Edward. He was on the island. But, to whom was he speaking?

Nicholas ran outside in the dark. He reached the end of the dock in front of the boathouse and jumped up and down. "Edward, Edward. Over here, it's me, Nicholas." His little voice echoed out over the water.

From out of the dark he heard, "Nicholas? Is that you? Where are you?"

"I'm here, over here on this dock!" Nicholas said.

"You stay where you are and I'll catch a ride in to you," Edward called back.

Nicholas could hear the low rumbling of voices speaking quietly. He heard the big bird splash and flap its wings again. Then, it was quiet. Suddenly, he could hear paddling and Edward's voice growing louder as he came closer. Out of the dark, a black bird emerged.

"Be careful now," Edward was saying. "Steady as you go. I don't want to get all wet, you know." A black-and-white speckled bird swam up to the dock. Its sharp beak snapped open, then shut, as if he was going to say something and changed his mind. Edward stood on the loon's back, holding on to its neck.

"Hello there, Nicholas," Edward said. "I've been hoping you would show up soon. I have news for you."

Chapter Twenty-Three

Nicholas was happy to see his friend again. With his help, they should find Francis and the journal soon. Before long, Nicholas thought, he would be heading home to his parents.

"Hello, Nicholas," Edward said. "This is my friend, Lewis. He has lived on this lake for years. He knows every cove, island, and rock along the shore."

"How do you do?" Nicholas said. "Edward, I am so glad to see you. I was silly to storm off to the coast. A horse named Betty brought me all the way up here from Portsmouth. We had quite a ride."

"Lewis, you must know just about everyone along the lake," Nicholas said. "Have you heard of my cousin Francis?"

"That's what I'm trying to tell you, Nicholas. While you were off horseback riding, I have been hot on the trail of Francis."

"Edward has been after me every day to make one more search of the lake," Lewis said. "I should have left for the coast long ago. But, we have a deal, don't we, Edward?"

"Well, that's right. Never mind the deal right now, Lewis. I have big news for you, Nicholas. I think I know where your cousin is. That is, I will know soon."

"Thanks to me," Lewis said.

"That's right," Edward said. "Lewis has found a clue, but I think I can solve it. We will follow Francis tomorrow."

"You found a clue?" Nicholas asked Lewis. "Where is it? What does it say?"

"Not so fast," Lewis said quickly. "Edward, we had a deal. I took you everywhere I could think of on the lake and you have to do something for me."

"All right," Edward sighed. "If I talk to her, will you help my friend and me?"

"That's the deal," Lewis said.

"Nicholas, my friend here wants me to speak to a certain lady loon down the lake."

"It's just that … you see, I am always so busy … I just want you to tell her about me, that's all," Lewis stammered and finally fell silent.

"Of course we will, Lewis," Nicholas said. "Where does she live?"

Lewis pointed with his wing down the lake. "She has a nest in the next cove down," Lewis said. "Don't tell her I sent you to talk to her. Just tell her about me." Lewis swam around in circles dipping his beak in the water and letting it run across his feathers.

Edward and Nicholas headed down the lakeshore, catching each other up on their travels. The sun rose behind gray clouds. They found the lady in question sitting alone on her nest. She sighed, looking up at the sky.

"Good morning, Madam," Edward said, bowing slightly. "I am Edward and this is my friend Nicholas."

"Hello," she sighed. "I'm Carol. It is very dreary this time of year. I should be off, I suppose. The lake will freeze soon. I just don't seem to have the energy."

As she spoke, Lewis paddled by offshore. He was doing his best to act as if he didn't see the other loon.

"Now we were just speaking to our friend there, Lewis. He was saying the same thing. He needs to head south, too. It can be a lonely trip, I understand."

Edward beckoned to Lewis. Edward made the introductions and he and Nicholas moved away. They watched from a distance as the two loons became acquainted. Nicholas saw Lewis flapping his wings. Carol flapped her wings back. In time, the two loons swam along the shore side-by-side.

"Ah, there you are, Edward," Lewis said. "Carol and I were just talking about heading to the coast for the winter. I believe I owe you a ride somewhere."

"How nice for you, Lewis," Edward said. "Yes, my friend and I will need a ride up to Tamworth. It's not too far out of your way."

"Tamworth?" Nicholas said. "What about the clue? I thought you said you knew where Francis was?"

"We need to visit my aunt and uncle in Tamworth. They will help us figure out the clue. Then we will know where Francis is. I am most sure of it."

The two birds floated in close to shore. Each animal climbed aboard a loon. The birds needed a long strip of water to become airborne. The loons paddled and paddled. They flapped their wings and swam through the water.

Edward, never happy flying, closed his eyes and held on tightly. Nicholas wiped the spray out of his eyes as the loons picked up speed. He liked to fly and knew the takeoff was the best part. With the island where

Lewis had his nest approaching, it was now or never.

Both birds strained to leave the water. Nicholas looked down as they became airborne. He could see into Lewis's empty nest.

"The clue," Nicholas shouted. "We forgot the clue." The clue lay in the nest, a pale gray stone among the small rocks and grasses. The birds, only looking at each other, flew up into the sky.

Chapter Twenty-Four

Nicholas looked down into Lewis's nest as they flew over. A flat stone, scratched with markings, lay against the grassy side of the nest. Without it, Nicholas would not be able to catch up with his cousin. He had to get Lewis to turn around.

"We need that stone," Nicholas shouted to Edward. "Lewis, we have to go back."

Lewis was busy gazing at his new friend. He flapped his wings and puffed out his white chest. "What's that, Nicholas? We're already late for our trip to the coast."

"But Lewis, I need that clue. Edward, tell him," Nicholas said.

"That was part of the deal," Edward said to Lewis. Edward held on tightly to Carol's neck.

"I don't know," Lewis said. "Carol and I are anxious to get away from this cold lake. Isn't that right, Carol?"

"Now, Lewis, if you told your friends you would do

something, you should do it. It will only take a few minutes," Carol said. Lewis couldn't resist Carol's red eyes.

"Oh, all right, if you think it's a good idea. Hold on, Nicholas," Lewis said. He banked hard and turned back toward his old nest. "I'm not going to land. It takes too much energy to take off again. I'll swoop in low and you grab the stone, Nicholas." Lewis skimmed low over the water.

"A little lower," Nicholas said. He held on to Lewis with one paw and reached down with the other. "We're almost there." Nicholas stretched as far as he could. As they flew over the nest, Nicholas's paw just swept over the granite stone. "I missed it," Nicholas shouted. Lewis was already climbing back into the sky.

Carol flew along behind Lewis. Edward, peeking out with one eye, groaned. He knew he would have to try. "All right, then," Edward said, screwing up his courage as best he could. "Carol, it looks like we are going to have to do it."

Carol flew low. The tips of her wings touched the water as she skimmed over the lake. Edward just leaned over a tiny bit. "You'll have to lean over more than that," Carol said. "I can't fly any lower."

Edward moaned and stretched out his paw. As they flew over the nest, Carol tipped to one side. Edward's paw touched the stone. He scooped it to his chest as Carol straightened up. From ahead, Nicholas cheered. "I knew you could do it, Edward," he shouted back to his friend.

Both birds rose into the sky heading north. Carol, with a chubby chipmunk and a granite stone, labored along. They left the lake behind. Ahead, mountains rose up to fill the landscape. Snow covered the peaks.

Edward, still amazed at the way he had grabbed the stone, took in the view. "Why, flying is not so bad after all, Nicholas," he said. "I believe I could get used to this sort of travel. Now, Carol, do be careful of those mountains ahead. What time will we be landing?"

"That's White Lake up ahead. I think we will land there. Those are the White Mountains you see in front of us," Lewis said. "Hold on, we're heading down now."

The two loons slid toward the water. They splashed into the water and glided to a stop near a sandy beach.

"Ah, there you go! Nicholas, hop down and follow me. We are near my aunt and uncle's home." Edward was ready to head toward the tall pine forest.

"Thank you for the ride," Nicholas said to Lewis and Carol. Edward stopped and turned around.

"Ah, yes, thank you for the ride. Did you see how I snatched that stone out of your nest, Lewis?"

"Yes, Edward, we all saw it," Lewis said. "Carol and I must be on our way." The two happy loons swam out onto the lake, took off, and headed east toward the ocean.

"They were very nice, don't you think?" Nicholas said. Edward trudged through the snow away from the water. "We must hurry, Nicholas. It is just starting to snow again. My aunt and uncle have a snug little burrow up among the pines."

Edward managed to carry the clue. Nicholas hurried along behind him. "We are looking for a big tree stump on the side of a steep hill," Edward said. Snow was falling fast now. They crossed a tarred road of White Lake State Park and plunged into the woods. They climbed a steep hillside.

"When they visited me in Plymouth last year, they said their house was in a big old stump on top of a granite ledge. It should be up here somewhere," Edward said. "It looks out over the lake."

Edward led Nicholas through the woods. The snow fell and the sun set. There were many granite ledges in the hillside. They rushed from stone to stone looking for the one with an old tree stump on top. Each time they were disappointed. It began to look like they would never find Edward's relatives.

Nicholas sat down in the snow. It piled up on his head. Edward, still carrying the clue, put it down and sat on top of it. They both chattered from the cold. If they sat there any longer, the snow would just cover them up.

A voice came out of the swirling snow. Someone was singing! Nicholas poked Edward and pointed. Out of the dark came a roly-poly chipmunk dragging a juniper branch with a cluster of berries still attached. The chipmunk stopped and looked at the two nearly frozen animals.

"Will wonders never cease?" the chipmunk said. "If it isn't my nephew Edward, sitting in my own backyard. Who's this with you? Come with me. I'll bring you home."

Chapter Twenty-Five

The wind howled and the snow swirled around the animals. They turned and followed Edward's uncle along the side of the hill. They came to a lump in the snow. Edward's uncle swept it clear with the juniper branch. A rotting pine tree stump emerged. In the middle was a carefully gnawed opening.

The plump chipmunk disappeared down the hole, dragging the juniper. Nicholas and Edward followed quickly. Inside the stump, the sound of the wind grew faint. All three animals shook the snow off their coats. They continued down into the snug burrow.

"Martha, I'm back, my dear. You will never guess who I found shivering at our door," the old chipmunk called out.

"Jeremy, there is no need to shout. I'm right here," an equally plump and smiling chipmunk called back. She stuck her head around a corner. "Well, my goodness, where on earth have you come from, Edward?"

"Hello, Aunt Martha," Edward said. "I was leading my young friend Nicholas to your home. And here we are."

"Yes, indeed," Jeremy said. "Here you are. It is a good thing I happened upon you two. Otherwise, you would be frozen out there until spring."

"Come here, Nicholas," Martha said. "Come warm up and have something to eat. Those two will go on for some time if we let them."

It was warm down here under the old stump. The air smelled sweet like pine resin. Bits of shredded cedar and pine bark lined the floor. It was a comfortable place for a mouse like Nicholas. When Edward and Jeremy came in, they all ate some of the juniper berries.

"Now then, you have eaten and have warmed up," Jeremy said. He stood and rubbed his paws. "Tell us, Edward, what brings you north this time of year?"

"It is this clue," Nicholas said. "I have been looking for my cousin Francis. He left clues and Edward said you would know what this one means."

"Ah, yes, the little mouse Francis. He had a map, journal, or something? Did he not?" Jeremy said. "We've talked about this before, Edward."

"That's right," Edward said. "Last year at Thanksgiving you told me about seeing Francis."

"The thing is," Nicholas said, "he left this clue behind." Nicholas held up the stone. "Can you tell us what it means?"

"Why, I am sure I can," Jeremy said. "Let me see

that." He took the stone. It was smooth and flat. The old chipmunk hummed to himself. To Nicholas it seemed like a long time. "It is a river stone, no doubt," Jeremy began. "It's granite for sure. This is called the Granite State, after all."

"It is the markings," Nicholas interrupted. "See, on the other side? Francis scratched in the stone."

"Ah, yes, I see," Jeremy said. "Quite unusual." Jeremy turned the stone over. He held it at arms length. "This could take some time to decipher."

"It looks to me," Martha said, "like the stone is in the shape of the state of New Hampshire. See, like this." She took the stone from Jeremy and turned it over one more time. She held it with the narrow end up and the wide end down.

"Of course," Jeremy and Edward said together. "It is obviously the state of New Hampshire."

"And these markings on one side," Nicholas said, "must be a map telling us where Francis was going?"

"Yes," Jeremy said. "It makes perfect sense now. What you have, Nicholas, is a map of New Hampshire telling you where Francis was going." Everyone looked at Jeremy. Jeremy cleared his throat. "Who would like dessert now? This snow won't let up for some time."

Nicholas and Edward spent the winter with Jeremy and Martha. The snow did let up, but a new storm came along every few weeks. When the animals ventured outside the stump, the deep snow made it hard to move. The forest had grown frozen and quiet. The world was at rest.

Most of the time, Nicholas stayed indoors. He studied the map and memorized the route. In the spring, they would have to leave the heavy stone behind and go after Francis. In the evenings, they listened to Jeremy tell old family stories. They all laughed at Edward's adventures from when he was young.

In time, the snow melted. Mountain streams roared to life. Wildflowers burst out of the thawed ground. Small animals arrived, blinking their young eyes in the bright sunshine. Edward and Jeremy took long walks over the muddy ground. They returned with freshly picked wild violets.

"We have returned with lunch for everyone," Edward said. "Help yourself, Nicholas."

"Edward," Nicholas said. "I think it is time we get going. The snow is gone. It has been a long time since we have searched for my cousin."

"I have come to love these mountains and the fresh clean air," Edward said. "I had almost hoped you had given up looking for Francis."

"My family at home is counting on me," Nicholas said. "I'm sure they are worried. I have to find that journal and get home. Now that the snow is gone, I should keep searching."

Edward looked at his aunt and uncle. "I had a wonderful time, but I did promise Nicholas I would stay with him until he found his cousin."

"That's right, Edward," Martha said. "Your friend needs you. You can visit again any time. Do you remember the route you have to take, Nicholas?"

"Sure," he said. "We have to get through the White Mountains and look for a little town on the edge of a river named for an old general. I wish I knew more about where we are going," Nicholas said.

"I am sure when we get up in the mountains this clue will make sense to someone. Things have a way of working out, don't they, Nicholas."

"I guess so, but they don't always work out the way you want them to."

Nicholas and Edward started north on what they hoped would be the last leg of their long journey through New Hampshire.

Chapter Twenty-Six

It was spring in the White Mountains. The trees sported tiny bright green leaves. Every day more songbirds returned from the south. Mountain streams, locked in ice all winter, bubbled in a rush downhill. Nicholas and Edward skipped along, happy in the sunshine. The ground, still damp from snow, felt warm under their paws.

They passed through small towns with big mountains. Ski trails on the mountains, covered in snow in the winter, were now grassy slopes. Nicholas and Edward hiked over each mountain. They would stop to eat tender wildflower stems and sit in balsam fir and red spruce trees along the edge of the trails.

From their high perch, the animals looked out at the range of mountains stretching on to the north and east. "Edward, how are we ever going to catch up with Francis?" Nicholas asked. "These mountains go on for ever and ever."

"You saw the map, Nicholas," Edward said. "We have to keep traveling north and find a way through."

"Are you looking for a way through the mountains?" a voice asked from overhead. "We can show you," it said. Two black-capped chickadees hung from a

branch. They looked down at the two small animals. "We know a way," they sang. Each bird hopped along the branch.

"We have been traveling for weeks. Whenever we make it to the top of a mountain, there is always another one to go over," Nicholas said. "We will never get through the mountains this way."

"You can't travel in a straight line in the mountains," one chickadee said. "My brother and I can tell you. I am Daniel. My brother is Evan."

"Tell us," Nicholas said. "How can we get through these mountains without climbing over each one?"

"You head for the notch, of course," Daniel said.

"The notch is a pass through the mountains," Evan said. "You have to go down to the valleys between the mountains. You could go through Crawford or Pinkham notches."

"I like Franconia Notch," Daniel said. "You know, where the 'old man' was?"

"The old man?" Nicholas asked. "Could he help us through the mountains?"

The chickadees chirped together. "It's not really an old man, it was a natural stone face that looked out over the mountains," Daniel said. "Some Native stories told how the stone face was once an Indian chief who was forever looking for his wife to return from the west."

"The stone face has fallen down," Evan said. "The old man is gone. They say his spirit has left the mountains and he is with his wife now."

"We are trying to find my cousin Francis," Nicholas said. "He is somewhere far in the northern part of the state."

"Yes," Edward said. "I don't want to turn to stone looking for him either. Tell us, which notch we should head for?"

The chickadees had found a deep crevice in the tree bark filled with insects. They pecked away at their lunch. "What did you say?" Daniel popped his head up, a small caterpillar dangling from his beak.

"We are looking for a small town named for a New Hampshire general, deep in the White Mountains," Edward said. "Can you tell us where that might be?"

"Let me see. Let me see," Daniel said. Evan continued to poke after the little insects. Daniel chirped and sang, trying to think.

"There's Stark," Evan said. "It's a little town near the very top of the state. Could that be it?"

"Of course, that must be it," Daniel said. "Stark is a little town on a river with a small library just right for a mouse to live under."

"How do we get there?" Nicholas asked. "We need to catch up with him quickly, before he moves on."

"Yes, it must be Stark," Evan said. "Keep Mount Washington on your left side. It is the biggest mountain in all of New England."

"Do we have to go over that one?" Nicholas asked. He had already had his share of climbing tall mountains.

"Well, if you want to, you could go up the Mount Washington Cog Railway," Daniel said. "It is a train that has been taking people to the top of the mountain since 1869. On a clear day, you can see four states, the province of Quebec, and the Atlantic Ocean."

"Well, it's not clear today and, even if it was, Francis is too small for us to see from there. I don't think we need any more side trips," Edward said. "Just tell us how to get to this little town of Stark, if you please."

"As I was saying," Daniel said. "You must pass through Pinkham Notch, go by Mount Washington, and then look for the town of Berlin. Stark is north of that."

"How long will all that take?" Nicholas asked. "This state seems to go on and on."

"Oh, not so long," Daniel said. "Not so long if you are flying, that is. I wouldn't want to have to walk."

"I bet Teddy will give them a ride," Daniel said. "You two wait here, we will go look for Teddy."

Daniel and Evan flew off. They left Nicholas and Edward wondering about Teddy. Who was he, and how would he give them a ride to the very northern part of the state?

Chapter Twenty-Seven

Nicholas and Edward didn't have to wait long to find out who Teddy was. Daniel and Evan flew in over the trees, chirping and chatting to each other. They landed again in a spruce. The branch bounced gently as they landed. A large shadow flashed past. A sharp-eyed black bird sat on another branch of the tree. It sagged under his weight.

"Are you the animals that need a ride to the Great North Woods," the raven croaked. It's long sharp beak and sleek black feathers gleamed in the sunlight.

"Nicholas and I, that is, we want to go to the North Woods," Edward stammered. "We need a way to get there as quickly as possible," he ended. The raven stared at them with his dark eyes. Daniel and Evan remained in the shadows under a branch.

"I have to find my cousin," Nicholas said. "He has a journal of my family's stories. I have to catch up with him and get it back. Can you help us?"

"I can't carry you both," Teddy said. "Which one of you will go and which will stay behind?"

"Oh, we both have to go," Nicholas said. "Edward and I have traveled together for so long. I couldn't go on without him."

"Now, Nicholas," Edward said. "You have to find your cousin. I, I, well, you know how I feel about flying," Edward said. The raven looked from one to the other.

"I will take you, Nicholas," the raven said. "Come, we must go now. It is a long flight."

Teddy, an impatient bird, caught Nicholas by the tail and flipped him onto his back. Commenting that he had business of his own, the raven lifted off the ground quickly. Nicholas looked down. Edward stood alone on the mountainside, waving his paws in the air.

The raven wasted no time. He didn't speak to the mouse on his back. He never mentioned the high peak of Washington as they flew by. Below, the cog railway chugged and puffed its way up the spine of the mountain. The great bowl of Tuckerman's Ravine and the Presidential Range passed without comment.

In time, the bird circled down among the mountains into a never-ending forest. He landed in a small town, made up of a library, church, and a school perched on the edge of a river. "This is Stark," Teddy said. "This is as far as I agreed to take you. Now hurry before I decide to make a meal out of you." The raven, hungry after his long flight, took a stab at Nicholas.

Nicholas ran fast, heading for a covered bridge that spanned the river. Teddy chuckled to himself. He made a half-hearted attempt to chase the mouse. He didn't want to fly into the covered bridge. The bird circled over the town, heading for the deep woods to the north.

Nicholas was alone in this little town. He peered out from the end of the bridge. He made a quick check of the sky to see if that awful raven was gone. He scurried out to make a search for cousin, as it was getting dark.

Nicholas looked at the library. It was a small building across the road. Nicholas sniffed around. "Francis," he whispered. "Francis, are you there?" In the quiet of the evening, he could hear the sound of animals rustling among the leaves behind the library.

The land rose up steeply. The wooded hillside loomed over the library and made the night even darker. Nicholas shivered. There could be almost any kind of animal in those woods. Most of them would find Nicholas a quick meal. He whispered sharply again, "Francis, is that you?"

The rustling stopped. From above him on the hillside, Nicholas heard someone call out, "Who is that? Who is calling for Francis?"

"Is that you, Francis?" Nicholas asked again. "I have been searching for you everywhere."

"My name is Percy," a mouse said, poking his nose out of pile of dried maple leaves. "Who are you?"

"I'm his cousin, Nicholas. Who are you? Is Francis with you?"

"You're his cousin?" Percy said. "He didn't mention he has a cousin."

"So you have talked with him?" Nicholas asked. "I need to find him. Does he have the journal?" There was a long period of silence. Nothing moved and no one said a word.

"How do you know about the journal?" Percy said. "That is supposed to be a secret. Francis will be mad."

Nicholas didn't know what to say. Of course he knew about the journal. It was his family's journal. Who was this mouse? Why was he hiding Francis, and how could Nicholas find his cousin and straighten out this whole mess.

Chapter Twenty-Eight

It didn't take long for Nicholas to get the answers to his questions. "If you are related to Francis, then he will want to see you. Follow me." Percy didn't wait for Nicholas to respond, but headed back up the steep hillside behind the library. The little mouse knew the way in the dark. Nicholas had to scurry along to keep up. They climbed higher and higher.

Granite ledges and tree roots poked out of the ground. The moon came out making it easier for Nicholas to see where they were going. The boulders, which had tumbled together when the mountains were young, made caves and hollows just big enough for a mouse. Soon they were high over the town.

Percy stopped on a round granite ledge. The Ammonoosuc River, sparkling in the moonlight, snaked its way through the valley. Nicholas tried to catch his breath and ask Percy how much farther they had to go. Before he could get the words out, Percy ran into a small cave. Nicholas followed.

When his eyes adjusted to the dark, Nicholas saw another small mouse hiding in the back of the cave. Percy was speaking to him in a whisper. The mouse was skinny and his fur was rough.

"Francis, I have found you at last," Nicholas said. He rushed forward to hug his cousin. "I have found your clues and have followed you all the way here. I have been on such a long journey, and now, here you are!" Nicholas chattered as he reached out his paws.

Francis shrank away from Nicholas. "What do you want from me? Why are you here? Where is my brother Sam? I left those clues for him. He was supposed to follow me here. What have you done to him?"

"I don't understand," Nicholas said. "I am your cousin. I didn't do anything to your brother. We met him but he headed off without saying where he was going. Francis, do you have our family journal?"

Francis looked at his cousin, and then he looked at Percy. "The journal is safe. It is my journal now and only I know where it is."

"That journal has our family stories in it," Nicholas said. "It doesn't belong to you or to me. We share it and should try to keep it safe together."

"I have it and only I know where it is. Besides, I am taking it to someone who will help me unlock the secrets inside."

"Francis, what are you talking about? The journal is only stories about our family. It doesn't have any secrets."

"We'll see about that," Francis said. "I am going to Vermont with it. There is a mouse I have heard about who knows all the true old histories. He will show me how to read the journal. I will find the secrets in it. I will be the one who will know everything."

Nicholas couldn't believe his ears. He had come so far looking for the journal. All he wanted was to bring it home safely to his family, all of his family. He didn't know what Francis meant by secrets in the journal. He stood in the cave looking at his cousin. Francis held his tail in his paws and sniffed at Nicholas.

Outside the night passed and the sun peaked over the hills on the other side of the river. A ray of light penetrated into the cave. Nicholas could see how worn and tired his cousin looked. He had traveled far, too. Francis had to carry the journal all this way alone. He had no one like Edward to help. "Francis," Nicholas said. "Tell me where the journal is and I will help you with it. I can help you take it to Vermont."

Francis dashed from the cave. Nicholas took off after him. Percy followed behind the other two. Despite looking worn out and tired, Francis moved quickly down hill. He tumbled in some spots and slid on leaves in other places. He never looked back. He landed with a bump behind the library.

Nicholas, following more slowly, didn't see where Francis went when he arrived at the bottom of the hill. Francis had ducked under the library building. Percy headed right for the spot where Francis had disappeared. Nicholas now followed Percy into the library.

Francis was high on a shelf in the single room of the small library. He was struggling with something wrapped in canvas. He pushed it to the edge of the shelf and shoved it over. The package landed with a thump next to Nicholas. The cover came off in a flap. It was the family journal. It was right here next to him.

Nicholas was stunned. Here was the book for which he had been searching for so long. The family stories, the history, everything he wanted to know about his past was right here in front of him. While he stood looking at the object of all his efforts, Francis scrambled down and swept it out of his reach.

He headed back out the hole he had come through. Nicholas couldn't believe it. One minute the journal was right there, and the next minute it was gone. Nicholas let out a cry and hurried after his cousin.

Outside, he could hear some scuffling around at the front of the library. Francis was shouting. Nicholas turned the corner of the building and there was Francis tugging on the journal and his friend Edward tugging it the other way.

"Edward," Nicholas shouted. "How on earth did you get here?" He ran up to his friend just as Edward yanked the journal free from Francis's grip.

"Hello, my friend. I rode up here with a lovely young doe. We just arrived when I ran into this mouse scurrying away with an old book," Edward said. "I believe you have been looking for this."

He handed Nicholas the journal. Here it was in his paws at last! Nicholas had done it. Thanks to Edward, here was the journal he had wanted for so long. He looked at Francis. His cousin was sitting on the ground. His head was down and he sniffed back a tear.

"Edward," Nicholas said. "I think we have to go to Vermont before we go home. Francis is part of my family. We need to help him. Francis, can we go to Vermont together? We can help you with the journal. We will help you unravel this story."

Francis rubbed his whiskers and sniffed back his tears. He was not alone anymore. "This river will take us out to the Connecticut River, which flows south all along the Vermont border," Francis said.

All three animals carried the journal to the water's edge. They found an old Tupperware container and shoved it into the water. They jumped aboard with the journal and bobbed out into the quick-moving current.

The three small animals would travel together. They would float down the river to the border. In Vermont, Nicholas, Edward, and Francis would search for the answer to the secrets hidden in the family journal.

mitten press

Mitten Press is proud to launch this series of chapter books about a lively field mouse from Massachusetts. He lives tucked under a farmhouse outside Stockbridge until a flood destroys the journal that contains his family history. In Book One, Nicholas embarks on a journey across Massachusetts to locate his long-lost uncle and a copy of the precious journal. Book Two sees Nicholas depart for Maine after finding out that his cousin has taken the journal copy there. As Nicholas will discover, Maine is a very large and diverse state. In this Book Three, Nicholas and Edward the chipmunk travel to the mountains of New Hampshire following a trail of clues left by cousin Francis.

The series will chronicle Nicholas's adventures throughout New England. In each book, young readers will learn about another state—the animals that live there, the geography, and even the state's history—as Nicholas continues his search for his family journal.

Coming soon …
Nicholas: A Vermont Tale
ISBN: 978-1-58726-522-8

Join Nicholas's New England Readers by sending your email address to the publisher at ljohnson@mittenpress.com. You will receive updates as new books in the series are completed and fun activities to challenge what you know about the New England states.